Cover Copy

One man, one muse, one romance to save the world

Immortal librarian Clio has existed for thousands of years. Her purpose—to influence and inspire mortals. Now as one has inspired her, a battle is mounting between the Muses and a god who care little for the plight of man. A hostile takeover is imminent at Olympus Enterprises.

History professor Jax Callahan is battling his own uncertainties. His previous employer's refusal to heed his warnings results in a tragic loss of life. Blaming himself, he no longer believes he can make a difference.

Tyranny will stop at nothing to appease her father and succeed in taking over Olympus and the world. To save mankind, Clio must reveal herself as a Muse to Jax, the man she's fallen in love with. Facing the end of humanity as they know it, she must convince him to trust in the magic of *what if*. Because failure spells doom for everyone.

Books by Gemma Brocato

Paranormal Romance
Mayhem Coming Nov 2016
Greed Coming Dec 2016

Contemporary Romance
The Five Senses Series
Cooking Up Love
Hearts In Harmony
Exposed To Passion
Bed Of Roses
Five Senses Shorts
A Winter Wedding
A Spirited Love
Playing With Fire

Romancing The Vine
Risking The Vine

Science Fiction Romance
Mission: Mistletoe

Tyranny

Goddesses of Delphi Book 1

Gemma Brocato

Copyright

Brocato, Gemma
Tyranny / Gemma Brocato
1. Romance—Fantasy. 2. Romance—Ancient Greek Mythology. 3. Paranormal—Romance—Mythology and Folk Tales

Dedication

For Joanne Wadsworth.
Thank you for encouraging me to take a leap with a
new genre.

Acknowledgements

Without help from many quarters, this book might never
have happened. My family: my publicity-shy husband,
whom I affectionately call Mr. Gemma, and my two
children, Erin and Andrew. You support me and cheer me
on and remind me of the good that happens when you share
a great love.

My editor, Corinne DeMaagd, whose patience and
mentoring as we worked on this story certainly qualifies
her for sainthood.

The KickAss Chicks and my Sassy sisters, you are all
strong, inspiring authors. I want to be just like you when I
grow up.

Author's Note

I have been intrigued by Greek mythology since I was quite young. Paintings and depictions of gods and goddesses have inspired great emotion and interest in me, making me want to learn more. So when I decided to write stories shrouded in mythology, it was natural to pick the Muses.

When I began researching the Muses I was struck by the myth of Pierus, and how he had nine daughters, like Zeus. Daughters, named the Pierides, he believed were superior to the Muses. So he goaded the Muses into a contest. When they won, to punish them for their insolence, Zeus transformed the Pierides into magpies. That legend became the basis for my stories. Nine muses, nine mortal men...nine chances at love to save the world.

The idea that Pierus would enter his offspring in a battle to take over Olympus evolved naturally. Every story must have a villain, right? Although, I frequently want to beat my head on the desk and wonder why I picked magpies? It's hard to find nine creative ways to portray the birds. Which is why I took a little poetic license in the naming of the birds. Should Pierus and crew ever win a challenge, all kinds of evil, which already exists in the world, would increase a thousand-fold.

It hasn't hurt that I love history...all kinds of history. So salting bits and pieces of the Muses backstory in through historical events made me smile. I hope you will find these little tidbits as much fun as I did.

I suppose this is where I have to say that any faults or errors in history are mine alone. Hey, if one of my Muses can face a magpie and win, then I guess I can own making mistakes.

Enjoy!
Gemma

Chapter 1

A violent crack of thunder rolled across the Allegheny mountains surrounding the Delphi City University Library. The boom reverberated off the elaborate stained-glass window in the marble stairwell. Clio Thanos hunched her shoulders, waiting for the flash of lightning to follow that would illuminate the impressive, colorful scene sculpted in the glass panels. Right now, the only impressive thing was it hadn't rattled right out of the lead beading that held the panels in place.

The storm was one of the worst Clio had ever experienced. And she'd lived through more than one lifetime worth of them. Rain pelted the stained glass like pebbles being tossed against a lover's window. The cavernous space of the Delphi City University library echoed back the pinging noise. The roar of pounding water echoed off the benign faces painted on the domed ceiling, as if the gods and goddesses depicted there were laughing out loud. Fanciful thinking. They never laughed, only bickered.

The storm had blown in with startling speed. One moment the noontime sun streamed in as soft light. The next, gloom shrouded the building. While the weather deteriorated, she headed to the concierge desk to help out. One of the student employees had called off sick, and Clio was the designated front-end back-up person today. Not that she ever minded staffing the entry. It was an opportunity to inspire students as they walked through the doors. Something she'd done without fanfare throughout each of her lifetimes.

Neither did she mind storms, but this one rated as particularly threatening. Thunder boomed with alarming regularity. The warm glow from the chandeliers dotting the room paled in comparison to the frequent blazes of lightning. Clio tensed after one blinding flash of clouds collided together, counting the seconds until the sonic roll followed.

As another rumble began, the heavy entry door flew open. From her position at the concierge desk, she noted the boiling black and gray clouds behind the entering student. The sharp scent of ozone assaulted her sinuses along with the earthy aroma of hot cement being pelted by torrential rain.

The young man wrestled the door closed, shutting out the storm. Drops of water flew out as the kid whipped back the hood of his sweatshirt. Ah, Brian. He was a library regular, the one with shaggy multi-colored hair. He showed up every day to study.

After shaking himself like a dog climbing out of a river, he shouldered his book bag. Splats of water dripped behind him as he approached the counter where Clio stood.

Using his sleeve, he slicked the rain from his face. "Jeez, it's literally raining cats and dogs out there."

"Literally or figuratively?"

"Huh?"

She almost laughed at his bewildered expression.

He shook more water from his shoulders. "It was sunny when I left the dorm. Not a cloud in the sky, then bam!"

His words echoed loudly. Clio held a finger against her lips. "Try to keep your voice down. You'll disturb the other patrons." The message lost a little—okay, a lot of—impact due to the fact she had to raise her voice above the thunder to deliver it.

He stopped digging in his backpack and raised mocking eyes toward her. "Really? You think anyone can concentrate in this racket?"

He left a tiny puddle of rainwater on the desk as he scanned in his ID card. While waiting for clearance to pass beyond the security gate, he smeared the moisture with his hand then blotted it up with the raggedy cuff of his shirt. In a sudden lull in the storm, the ping of the monitor sounded, jolting the kid into action. Using his hip, he nudged open the now unlocked swinging gate. His Vans sneakers squeaked as he disappeared between two massive bookshelves.

Judging by the diminished sounds on the windows, it seemed the freak summer storm had lessened. Clio jerked a cleaning rag from under the counter and swiped the remaining water from the marble countertop. Double-checking to ensure her entry badge remained clipped to her belt, she slipped from behind the desk. The swinging gate creaked as she pulled it toward her to sidestep through.

She dropped the towel to the floor, and with the toe of her sandal, mopped up the wet footprints Brian had left in his wake. Once she finished that chore, she mentally commanded her face to relax, erasing the scowl tightening her muscles. The tension that had arisen with the sudden tempest eased as she walked to the nearest wall-mounted safety cone holder adjacent to the entry door. She hooked a finger in the nylon pull-tab and tugged. The cautionary cone swung free and popped open, bumping against her thigh.

Now she just had to figure out the best spot for the

wet-floor warning. As she pivoted, the heavy wooden entry door swept inward again. A sudden gust of wind caught the door and propelled it toward Clio's head. The dull *thunk* of the door connecting with her forehead rebounded in her ears. Glittering stars burst behind her eyes.

She stumbled backward, arms flailing. The safety cone flew from her grasp.

"Mother goddess!" The epithet burst from her lips before she could bite it back. Tears watered her vision as a large man reached for her. His big, warm hand wrapped around her arm and steadied her. A barrage of tiny, invisible arrows traveled from his fingertips up her arm.

"Oh, God! I'm so sorry. Are you okay?" When he spoke, his husky baritone voice vibrated through her chest.

She rubbed the tender spot on her head and blinked to clear the moisture from her eyes, bringing the man into focus.

Set under a pair of slashing brows, deep amber eyes reflected warmth and concern. A sexy scruff of midnight black whiskers covered a square jawline. His lips thinned and turned down in a frown. She took a step away, breaking the hold he had on her arm, and immediately missed the heat and comfort.

His broad shoulders, encased in a blue oxford cloth shirt, were wet from the rain. Drops of water sparkled on his cheeks and eyelashes. He probed his thumb over her forehead, gingerly testing the sore spot and rising lump there. When she flinched, he did as well.

She pushed his hand away. "I'm okay. I keep asking the administration to install glass entry doors to avoid things like this happening. Perhaps if I have a concussion, they'll listen."

"Oh, hell! Did I hit you that hard?"

She shook her head cautiously to make sure her brain didn't rattle around. "No, I exaggerated."

As much as it grieved her to do so, she turned from the

man's gaze and stooped to retrieve the wet floor sign. A moment later, she'd settled the bright yellow cone over a damp spot on the floor. Her thoughts still on the man next to her, she spun around to return to her work area. As she slipped on a slick spot, the stranger reached for her once again. One arm around her waist, the other grasping her arm, he kept her upright, balancing her against his solid body. He saved her from a mortifying tumble to the floor. Although, if he were a cushion, she'd gladly take a fall if landing on him was part of the cost. Preferably straddled on his lap.

And where in Zeus's name had that thought come from?

As he steadied her on her feet, again, she shook the sexy, errant thought away. "Thanks."

"My pleasure."

Ooh, that deep voice rasped across her senses in a deliciously wicked way, making her imagine all sorts of things strictly forbidden by library policy.

The heels of her sandals clicked sharply on the floor as she moved across the vestibule. The rain had stopped as quickly as it had started, and the soft click of the security lock disengaged as she swiped her badge over the scanner. The ancient marble counter was cool when she laid a palm on it and turned the corner to resume her station behind the desk.

Mystery man faced her across the desk. His shirt, two buttons open at the throat, revealed smooth, taut skin, a healthy shade of tan, as if the man spent hours in the sun. He rested one hand on the counter between them, the other wrapped around the strap of a tattered messenger bag.

The sight of his long fingers and the muscle on the side of his hand made her gut twist in an odd, delicious way.

"May I help you?" Clio inquired in her most professional voice.

"I'm new on campus and was told I need to register

here for research privileges."

"You're a grad student?" Funny, he looked older than typical doctoral students.

"No, actually, I'm a professor. I'll be teaching comparative civilizations to undergrads who think they're taking an easy A class. Love to catch them unaware." He rubbed his hands together and flashed even white teeth in a maniacal grin. A deep throaty chuckle followed as he slipped his hand into his back pocket and withdrew his wallet.

He had a nice, warm laugh, the kind she'd love to hear again and again. She accepted the ID card from his hand.

Jax Callahan. Assigned to the history department at DCU. His badge was coded with the usual gibberish lines only a barcode reader could decipher. Clio pulled the nearest keyboard toward her and tapped the space bar. Once the screen flared to life, she entered in her passcode.

She navigated through a couple of screens until she found the information she sought. Sliding her gaze from the screen, she smiled at Professor Callahan. "This will just take a moment."

He dropped his eyes to the name badge clipped on her thin silk blouse. "Take your time, Clio." He relaxed against the counter, leaning one elbow on the stone and letting his glance wander around the library. "Holy hell, would you look at that ceiling? It's like the freaking Sistine Chapel in here."

Clio tossed a look above her head at the paintings on the ceiling. Used to seeing it every day, she mostly ignored the familiar faces staring down on her. But she understood why the newcomer was in awe. The colorful scenes above them truly did rival the famous work in the Sistine Chapel, except many gods lived here, versus the single deity Michelangelo had painted in Rome.

Hiding a tiny smile behind her curtain of her red hair, Clio waved the small rectangle of plastic under the crisscrossed red beams of the scan gun affixed to one side of the monitor. After a slight hesitation, the machine began populating the on-screen form.

"Excuse me, Ms. Library Lady. The computers are down." Brian approached the side of the desk. The servers dedicated to the library's collection frequently went down in bad weather. Thankfully, the administrative system was independent of the online catalog.

"Give it a minute, Brian. They'll be back online shortly."

"Got a class soon, can't wait. Can you tell me where to look up when the Greek War of Independence was fought? Man, this class sucks. I knew I shouldn't have registered for summer school."

Clio gave the kid a sunny smile. "The war ended in 1828 when Ioannis Kapodistrias became the Governor of Greece. He was assassinated in 1831 and his brother, Augustinos, assumed power."

The student twisted his mouth to the side. "Did you just make that up?"

"No…" *Oh goddess.* "It's common knowledge."

The kid squinted his eyes and curled his upper lip. "Yeah, maybe in Greece, but where would I find that information here?" He swept his arm around to indicate the library.

Heat flushed up her cheeks. Her problem was that she always knew the answer but forgot to cite a source. She grabbed a piece of paper and scrawled the Dewey number of the book the kid needed. "Second floor, ancient civilizations room, fifth stack from the door, about midway down on the third shelf." She skipped mentioning the book was red as she pushed the paper across the counter. Narrowing her eyes, she gave him a mental nudge, the kind that had inspired countless others to take matters into their own hands.

That was her true purpose…to inspire others to

creativity. And this kid needed all the influence she could spoon-feed him.

His gaze faltered as he took a step back, clutching the slip of paper. "Thanks." The kid's tennis shoes still squished on the marble floor as he hurried away. Clio shook her head, glanced at the computer, then at Professor Callahan.

Who stared at her as if she'd sprouted a second head. The skin between his brows had puckered.

Impatiently, she pushed a lock of hair back from her face. "What?"

"How'd you do that?"

"Again, what?"

He rapped his knuckles on the sleek cream and gray countertop. "I teach history, and it would have taken me at least five minutes to dig that answer from my brain. Honestly, I'm not even sure I could do that without resorting to the Internet to find the information you just spewed like it was your address."

"I looked it up," she deflected.

A shock of his black hair flopped into his eyes as he shook his head. "Hmm, no you didn't. Computers are down, remember?" He scratched the backs of his fingers over the stubble on his cheeks. The resulting noise was…pleasing.

Busted. Dammit, why hadn't she faked she had to look it up? The easy answer was she was too distracted by the immediate attraction she felt for this absolute stranger. Too distracted by the appealing professor to hide the fact she'd chronicled many senseless atrocities over the millennia.

She bit her lip and cast her eyes down. How did she tell someone she'd just met she possessed the special, mystical powers that came with being a Muse? She didn't. Her secret had been safe from mortals for thousands of years.

She debated lying and telling him she'd been a history

major. Nah, he'd never buy that story. Her online credentials, which anyone could access, showed her as a Master of Library Science. The urge to confide her secret to this man whipped around her belly like a dog chasing its tail. The idea took her by surprise. In all her lifetimes, she'd never wanted to reveal her role as a Muse to a single mortal.

Grasping the wireless mouse, she concentrated on the computer screen. It would be much easier to lie if she didn't look at him. She reached out with her gift and nudged him to leave it alone. "I have a photographic memory. I must have seen it in some book and remembered." The lie tasted sour on her tongue. "Ah, here you are. Professor Callahan. Oh, wow! You have full research and facility privileges."

"No one can remember details like that. It's not possible."

Wait a minute. How could he resist her subtle mental push? Maybe he required a slightly stronger nudge to redirect his train of thought. "Your credentials really are impressive."

His eyes turned cloudy and confused, and his brows needled together. He shifted his weight from one foot to the other. "Why impressive?"

Clio eased out a relieved breath. On the second try, she'd been able to distract him from her spewage of facts that would have required extensive research from most mortals, the sexy professor included. But it shouldn't have taken two tries. Normally, a single nudge was sufficient. She'd never felt the need to bash a mortal over the head with suggestion. Some of her sisters had, but she'd been happy to offer quiet influence. A niggle of concern rose, but she squelched it before it could bloom into doubt.

She jerked the mouse to an on-screen option and clicked to the bit of his personnel file she was allowed to check. "Full access is something typically reserved for department heads and deans. I don't see either of those positions on your account." How in the hell did he score this little perk? Facility access meant he could be in the library after hours with only a security guard in attendance. Only she and a handful of other people had that privilege.

The light surrounding Jax faded. Oppressive gloom reclaimed the interior of the library. Thunder boomed again, startling Clio into a tiny jump. The noise and his unexpected access raised her suspicions along with the hair on the back of her neck. Something was wrong.

Her cell phone rang quietly with the tones of a calliope. The ring tone she'd set for her sister Callie. The tinny, hollow music sealed her premonition that something was out of sorts in the universe.

She held up one finger, signaling Jax to sit tight, and grabbed her phone. She tapped the Answer button. "Callie, I can't talk now."

"Then just listen. We have trouble. Meeting tonight at The Rowan Tree. Eight sharp. Do not be late this time or history will be repeating itself."

Damn her perfectionist sister. Clio had been late once—one single time—and Calliope had never let her live it down. It really wasn't Clio's fault she'd lost track of time while recording history. She'd been doing her job. To make up for her tardiness, she'd bent over backward and gave into her sister's demands for help on some research. That had been twenty hours of life Clio would never get back.

God, it sucked to be a pleaser. She told Callie, "I'll be there. Gotta run." She disconnected, mentally flipped off her overbearing sister, and faced Jax again.

He watched her with a degree of fascination she'd never witnessed in this lifetime. Or any other. A sexy gleam danced in his eyes. "So, my privileges…"

"Right." She groped in the hanging file under the desk. As she drew out the info sheet he needed, she smacked the back of her hand on the hard marble underside of the counter. Shaking off the sting, she slid the list of privileges and his ID badge across the surface toward him.

He grasped her hand and stroked his thumb over her knuckles. "You seem destined for injury today."

Oh, goddess, the motion of his thumb invoked crazy, sexy thoughts. *Focus, Clio.*

She ignored the erotic sensation and pulled her hand from his. She tapped the paper. "This will tell you everything you need to know. Your employee number is your after-hours access code. Just key it in to the PIN pad next to the front entrance. Once you're through the entry protocol, the security officer on duty will scan your badge for admittance to the library."

"Regardless of what time?"

"Yep. Your access is coded for twenty-four-seven."

"And what hours might I find you here?"

His smile carved dimples into his cheeks like an ancient sculptor who had etched lines into a block of marble. Pleasure fluttered to life in her belly. He was flirting. Her finger twitched with the need to trace the lines around his mouth. "I'm here during normal business hours."

Jax leaned over the counter and lowered his voice. "What if I need a research assistant? You know your history. Are you available after hours?"

Was he asking her on a date? Or was she just wishful thinking? She tipped her head to the side, as if she'd be able to see into his head from that angle. "I'm always happy to help."

He flicked his rich brown eyes to her lips, then back up. "I'll remember that." He straightened and dragged the strap of his bag back up his shoulder. Once it was situated, he pocketed his ID. The motion caused his damp shirt to stretch against his broad chest. He folded the guide sheet she'd given him into thirds, thirds again, and then slipped it into the back pocket of his jeans. He sauntered away from her with one last grinning glance over his shoulder. God, his smile was killer.

Chapter 2

I n the four hours that had elapsed since he'd met her, Jax Callahan hadn't been able to get Clio Thanos from his mind. After his visit to the DCU library, he'd stopped at the student union for a bite to eat.

Leaning his back against the brick wall of the dining room, he mused about how silky her skin had felt under his fingertips when he kept her from falling. How his dick had twitched to life when he'd steadied her against his chest. On a heat scale of cold-as-ice to fucking-incendiary, his last affair had been only tepid. Mere casual contact with Clio's body far exceeded what he'd had with a woman whose face he barely remembered. To be fair, he doubted that woman remembered him either. He'd been in the midst of a career meltdown at the time. Not a shining moment in his past.

Thoughts of the alluring redhead he'd just met continued to dominate once he returned to the office. Littered with boxes of his possessions, things he'd been unpacking for days, the tiny space was snug and tight, just the way he envisioned Clio might feel around his cock. As blood rushed to his groin, jeans that had fit just fine this morning were suddenly too damn tight.

Hoping to gain control of his unruly body, he burst from the rickety office chair, banging his knee on an open drawer. Son of a bitch! At least pain was an effective boner killer.

With a disgusted snort, he opened the box sitting atop

his desk. Right at the top was the candle his mom had given him to help "spruce up" his new office. She was a big fan of things that smelled good. Prying off the lid, the cinnamon aroma wafted in his face. An instant flashback took him to the precious moments he'd stood across the counter from Clio. She smelled of cinnamon and citrus. The warm, homey scent reminded him of presents and Christmas.

He'd like to unwrap her, starting with the silky gold blouse with the pearl buttons and making his way to the sleek black skirt. But he'd leave the high-heeled sandals on her feet. Her toenails had been painted cherry-red, and a sexy little toe ring had winked in the glow cast by the chandelier in the entry foyer of the library.

Holding the candle to his nose, he shut his eyes and imagined the color and style of her undergarments. He pictured her in lace and satin, in the same shade as on her toes. Or electric blue like her eyes. He let his imagination wander to stripping the scraps of fabric off her lithe body and laying her on a plush bed. Would she taste like cinnamon when he went down on her? The pain in his knee forgotten, his shaft thickened and lengthened as he imagined her juicy, ruby-colored slit. Inhaling the cinnamon scent of the candle again, his ball sack tightened.

Loud thumps sounded on his office door a second before it swung open. "Hey, Jax. What's up?"

He slammed the candle down on the desk. Thank God, he stood behind a stack of boxes.

Ian Sommers stepped into the cramped space, a broad smile on his square face. He whistled as he scanned Jax's new digs. "Dude, they found the smallest office on campus for you."

Ian had been a friend since grad school, although he'd majored in science, not history. The man worked for a large pharmaceutical company based in Delphi. His old friend's presence in town had been the deciding factor in accepting the teaching position with the university instead of staying with his former employer, a prestigious Washington think tank. Burned out on the prospects for the future of civilization, his decision had been easy.

Jax eased his weight onto one hip and, behind the cover of the box, adjusted his hard-on to a more comfortable spot. "Hey, Ian. Just getting settled in. You slumming today?"

Ian threw himself into the low-backed leather chair across the desk. He dangled his hands over the padded armrests. "I had some vacation days coming, and there isn't much going on with my research project this week. We're between phases. My research assistant can handle the miniscule amount of work necessary. I took the afternoon off to see if I could get you on the courts for a game of tennis. Too bad the weather isn't cooperating. Want to go get a brew and watch the ball game instead?"

Jax gazed out the grimy window. Gray clouds scuttled across the sky, but at least it had quit raining. Weak light glared off the scattered puddles dotting the street. "Tempting, but I can't today. I really need to get settled in here." He rested his hands on his hips and shifted his focus to the cluttered room.

Ian tipped his head back and laughed. He combed his fingers through his shaggy blond hair, pushing it back from his face. "Yeah, your words say I'm a worker bee, but your expression says crap-I'd-kill-for-a-beer."

"Sorry."

"Classes don't start for another month." Ian's voice took on a familiar wheedling tone. "Come on. Play hooky with me, just like the old days when we blew off classes to race jet skis on the reservoir."

Jax's resolve crumbled. "Those were the days, weren't they? Sun and wind and sweet young co-eds to keep us company." His tastes ran more refined now—candles, a comfortable mattress, and a certain redhead came to mind.

He closed the lid of the box in front of him. "You're right. This can wait. My gaming system is operational. Wanna grab some take-out and play World of Warcraft?"

"Hell to the yeah!"

Jax tossed the eighteen-speed bike he'd ridden to work this morning into the back of Ian's ancient green Land Rover for the fast trip back to his house. He settled in the passenger seat, fondly recalling Ian's excitement over finding the truck and the hours they'd spent restoring it. He drew a fingertip across a scar on the back of his hand. He'd sliced it open trying to help re-install the rehabbed engine. The pain had been worth it. The speedometer only went as high as seventy, but Ian had pegged it more than once.

On the way home, they hit up the drive-through at a clog-your-arteries fast food place for burgers and seasoned fries. After Jax grabbed beers from the fridge, they settled in front of the top-of-the-line behemoth of a television. That sucker dominated one entire wall in the living room. While they ate, Jax tuned the channel to the baseball game. Sixth inning and the Delphi Demons had a dominating seven-run lead. They were at bat with two men on and no outs. It was gonna be a blow out. Jax switched to the 24-hour news station on the TV.

Ian protested. "Hey, I wanted to watch the game."

"News flash, the Demons are going to win.

"Yeah, but I like to bask in the reflected glory."

"So bask already." Jax lifted his bottle and took a sip. Hoppy flavor danced on his tongue.

"You know, buddy, I'm glad you decided on Delphi, but I'm not sure why you traded the glamour of DC for a second tier university." Ian chomped on a huge bite of his loaded burger. A blob of ketchup plopped onto the table. Ian swept it up with a finger and scrubbed it away with his napkin.

"Don't sell DCU short. It's a great university."

"Maybe, but it doesn't move or shake like the DC

dance." Ian shimmied in his seat, bringing a reluctant grin to Jax's face.

"I told you I don't need the drama of dealing with politicians and their incessant posturing. I could talk to them until I was blue in the face, and they'd never understand why repeating history would be a huge mistake." Jax shook his head and contemplated his beer. "You have to be partially insane, or maybe wholly insane, to want to work in that kind of environment."

"It does take a special breed of cat. But maybe by being in the tank with the other sharks you could bring sanity. No one understands historical nuances better than you."

Understanding and being able to effectively communicate why certain strategies would be a mistake were two different things. Since Jax's expertise was with the former, not the latter, he knew he'd simply spin his wheels. The influential people had stopped listening to the advice he offered.

He wadded up the wrapper from his burger and dropped it into the bag by his feet. "They ignored my warnings and advice regarding The Five Nations Block shenanigans. You know how that ended." With the genocide of thousands of ethnic civilians who'd squatted in disputed territory near the Black Sea. Tension rose up Jax's neck, the sensation cold, clammy, and fierce. He rolled his shoulders. "No thanks. I don't need the headache."

Ian pegged him with an earnest look. "Think what the outcome could've been if you'd kept fighting, man."

"Ian, if I'd kept fighting, it would have been my picture in the dictionary next to the definition of insanity. New problems, same result. What good is giving advice if they don't listen?" Shame and guilt climbed his chest as he recalled the one time they had listened and his advice had been wrong. He still ached for the lives that had been lost in the blood diamond fields in Sierra Leone.

"Bastards." Ian's tone was laden with derision.

Loud laughter burst from Jax. "Yeah, they are."

"You've done a great job getting set up here." Ian had helped move boxes from the rental truck into Jax's house, but had bailed on unpacking. He wiped his fingers on a napkin. "You still have the best home theater system I've ever seen."

Stupid, juvenile pride swelled within his chest. Only the best surround-sound speakers would do for him. The sub-woofer thumped out the bass and rocked a body good. "It keeps me occupied. Not much to do most nights, so I've been concentrating on gaming and defeating pretend enemies."

"We need to fix that sad state of affairs, dude. I'd be happy to set you up on a blind date. I know a couple of fun girls who'd die to go out with you."

"Not much into blind dates." The only woman he wanted to date had stunning red hair, vivid blue eyes, and freckles sprinkled across her nose. "I did meet someone interesting today. Do you know Clio Thanos?"

Ian's eyes glittered speculatively in the reflected glow from the television. "Super-cute librarian Clio?"

He forgot sexy. Sexy, flame-haired librarian Clio. "Obviously you know the woman. What's her story?"

Ian scrubbed his jaw. "She has a photographic memory to go with her rocking bod."

So Ian knew about her freaky fast ability to pull information from her internal memory banks. "I was impressed when she gave a student an answer without looking anything up. And she delivered correct information. It was about Greek government, one of my specialties, and I doubt I could have come up with the answer as fast as she did."

"You hot for her? I mean, you could do worse. But I'm warning you—ya gotta get by her sisters to date her. The whole Thanos clan is tight and closed off."

"Spoken like a man who's run afoul of them in the past."

"Dude, there are nine siblings in that family. Every single one of them a female. I've had some dealings with one of her sisters, Polly." Ian's tone heated up. "She's an investigative reporter for Channel Seven."

"Hmm, there's a story there."

"Yeah, but we aren't talking about me. So, Clio…" Ian circled his hand.

"Not much to say except she intrigued me. I met her when I went to set up my research access. Apparently, I have some…privileges that impressed her. I have twenty-four-seven access to the whole building."

Ian whistled low. "The DCU administration rarely grants full privileges. I've been petitioning them for the past year for access to their science library. I'm a goddamn PhD, and they won't give me the time of day."

Jax's shirt drew tight across his back when he shrugged. "What can I say? I must have the necessary clout. Now I have to find a way to make Clio want whatever it is that makes me so damn special. I predict I'll be spending a lot of time at the library in the near future." He'd like to spend some time in Clio's bed as well. He'd have to work on the details of that quest. Hopefully it wouldn't end up an exercise in futility—the way his assignment to the GeoPoly think tank had been.

"Well, good luck with scoring a date with her. Let me know how you fare. I'll have some other options lined up for you in case you don't get past hello."

While Jax collected their rubbish, Ian flipped the channel back to baseball and seemed to have forgotten about the Thanos sisters. Jax pitched the grease-stained bag into the trash, grabbed two more beers, and rejoined Ian on the leather sofa in front of the television. He wrangled the remote from Ian's hand. He swiped his thumb over the control pad, logging on to the state-of-the-art gaming system.

Jax wished his attraction to Clio came with the same kind of simple control, one he could turn on and win her interest. She intrigued him, made him want to know more about her. Their shared interest in history would be a good spot to start in developing a relationship with the woman. As it stood, the woman had already gotten under his skin the way no woman had in…ever. And it appeared he'd be content to let her stay there, at least until he found a way to scratch that itch.

Chapter 3

"Calliope, this is the second time in a month you've called us together for an emergency meeting." Clio used her sister's given name to irritate the woman, and for good measure put air quotes around the E-word as she slid onto the bench opposite her sister. The last time Callie summoned them was the day of the violent storm, when Clio first met Jax. "For a feeling? We have to have something more concrete than there's a disturbance in the force."

Callie rolled her eyes and slouched against the wooden back of the booth. "So funny, Clio Schlemiel."

Exasperation churned inside Clio. She'd hated Callie's nickname ever since she'd first rolled it out when they were teens. She was not awkward, or unlucky. Thankfully, Callie was the only sister who dared to continue calling her that after Clio had a fit about it. Since they'd been born eight millennia earlier, Calliope had always been the leader of the pack, leaving Clio to quietly plod along as a middle sister.

"Who else is coming tonight?" Clio was the second to arrive. They were in a smaller booth, which meant some of the Muses wouldn't be present.

"Just Polly and Nia." Callie chewed her lower lip while she eyed the front door.

They were meeting at The Rowan Tree, their preferred pub when a meal had to be involved. None of them cooked.

Domestic arts seemed to be the only area where they lacked inspiration. Kind of funny, given their roles as Muses.

Callie's focus was the written word. Over the millennia she'd inspired Homer, Dante, Shakespeare, and countless others. She seemed most proud of her achievement with Harper Lee. It had been Callie's idea to include Boo Radley as a character in *To Kill a Mocking Bird*, a fact she'd repeatedly crowed about.

Polly, or Polyhymnia, was the Muse of Sacred Song. Over the years, her focus had shifted from inspiring prayers and hymns to making sure correct information about all manner of *stuff* got disseminated accurately. Her job as an investigative reporter had been essential in breaking several high-level scandals and plots. Without her influence, Clio knew countless Ponzi schemes and blatant book-cooking episodes wouldn't have been exposed.

Urania, or Nia, had kept her head in the clouds throughout all her incarnations. Nia was the Muse of the Heavens. Her job at the Helios Institute and Observatory fit her like a glove. Without Nia's influence and carefully cultivated inspiration, there wouldn't have been a Mars Rover or a Hubble Telescope. Nia's humble deflection of her accomplishments was epic in their family. All she wanted was to allow mortals to see in deep space what she saw without the aid of technology.

A spot in Clio's heart warmed as her little sister walked into the slightly darkened interior of the bar. Nia's copper-penny bright hair glittered with moisture from the fine mist that had settled over Delphi in the last few weeks. The recent weather had been extremely.

Actually, ever since the day they'd had the summer squall. The day Jax Callahan had bumped into her life. He'd been into the library six times in the last two weeks. Each time he'd invited her to accompany him as his research assistant. Each time, she'd declined. But he'd remain at her desk, chatting—flirting, really—finding any excuse to touch her. Her skin sizzled each time he brushed her arm or shoulder. Each touch had her nerves jumping like water in a hot skillet.

She was certain he was working his way up to asking for a date. The way he pinned her with those whiskey-colored eyes, or flashed his dimpled smile at her… Goddess, he embodied walking, talking lust.

And she was to the point of thinking they should have sex first, then maybe think about dating later. Her most intimate spot, her brain, had started firing the second he walked through the library doors. Other parts of her anatomy had tingled in anticipation as well.

"Hey, chicas." Nia slid onto the bench seat right next to Clio, distracting her from the X-rated thoughts of Jax. "What gives with the weather?"

Callie drew her brows together, puckering double lines in the center. "The weather is symptomatic of a larger problem. I've been getting cryptic e-mails over the last two weeks."

Clio gusted out a frustrated breath. "Callie, why didn't you say something earlier?" Like the last time they were together, when her emergency meeting had been nothing more than helping Callie brainstorm her way out of a plot hole.

Her sister's shrug irked Clio, but she'd learned a very long time ago not to press.

"Let's wait until Polly gets here. I don't want to have to repeat myself," Callie said.

"What's new, Clio?" Nia asked while she consulted the menu.

A desperate attraction to a sexy man. An overwhelming urge to crawl between the sheets with said man, and not crawl out for days. "Nothing much."

A waitress approached the table. After ordering, Nia said, "Well, let me tell you what's new in my life. I finally managed to get the bozo engineer at NASA to aim the

Hubble in the right direction. They are all atwitter about a new nebula that somehow, miraculously, managed to pop up. Like it hadn't been there all along. I didn't think he'd ever learn."

Clio beamed at her sister. "Congrats! How long have you been working on him?"

"For. Ever!" Nia exaggerated. Forever in their lives was a very, very long time. "I must have nudged for at least a week."

Still frowning, Callie drummed her fingers on the table and squirmed in her seat.

Before Clio could respond, Polly raced up to the table. She jostled Callie as she dropped onto the bench. "Sorry I'm late. Traffic was killer. Damned rain." She shoved her fingers through her damp tresses.

Callie waited until after the waitress had taken Polly's order before starting the meeting. She pulled a sheaf of papers from her bag and handed them around. "This is the latest e-mail I've gotten. I've been getting little teasers over the past two weeks. The top one, received today, spells everything out. I've tried to track them to their source, but the messages hop all over the world before they reach my inbox." She pinned each of the girls in turn with a look meant to impart the importance of the message. "I think the e-mail and the weather are connected. Read them."

Silence ruled the table. Clio scanned the paper, then read again more slowly.

The time is nigh. Your fates are sealed. The existence you've known for the millennia is at an end. Nine challenges for nine Muses. Each Muse will pair with a mortal man to solve the test. No need to look for your challenge partner. He will find you. But he will not be predisposed to your cause. A kiss will seal your partnership, but it will also free my daughters' wings. To win, you must get this man to reject a deep-seated belief. To save your precious world, this man must ask, "What if? "

*If even one Muse fails the test, all fail. But I have
decided you must continue the challenges for a chance to
redeem all humankind. For each defeat, one of my
daughters will be released from her existence as a magpie.
An existence forced on my offspring at the order of your
father, Zeus. The defeated Muse will then transform into
the magpie with no chance of redemption. And when my
daughters obtain freedom, havoc will come. The world will
once again belong to the gods, not to the humans.*

*Your challenges begin now as warrior men rampage
once more. Look to The Five Nations Block as the bringer
of authoritarianism.*

"Signed by Pierus." Polly smacked a palm on the table.
"I knew that dirt-bag couldn't stay quiet forever."

Clio's world spun as she recalled the evil god who'd
put his daughters above the Muses. His actions had
angered Zeus, her father, so much that he'd turned the
daughters to magpies. But after witnessing Pierus's grief at
the loss of his offspring, Zeus had relented enough to allow
Pierus to petition for their release. Sort of an Olympian
parole.

Over the millennia, Pierus had challenged the Muses
repeatedly in an attempt to release his daughters from the
bird form they'd been condemned to by the supreme ruler
of the gods. He'd failed each time. But that didn't stop him
from trying to resurrect a centuries old beef every once in a
while. Clio still got exhausted when she thought about the
first. The challenge was to travel around the globe in under
a year without using supernatural powers to transport
themselves. They'd nearly lost when they spent several
weeks turned around in the South China Sea. Thankfully,
Nia had already inspired the inventor of the compass.

And each time he surfaced, the Muses had worked
hard to beat him. If at any point they'd lost, the fate his
children represented would have been released. And with

daughters with names like Tyranny, Strife, Hate, Greed, the world would become a very evil place if the Muses failed.

She put a hand to her forehead, hoping to ease her sudden dizziness. "It's like a freaking terminal case of déjà vu. How many times have we already proven we're better than his brats? Why is he re-challenging us now?"

Callie shrugged. "Pierus must see something we can't. Know something about world events we don't. His ticket to rescuing his evil spawn."

"If one of us fails the contest, all fail? That's new. What the hell?" Nia's blue eyes held a hint of panic. She took a big gulp of wine and swallowed hard.

"We won't fail," Polly barked. The fork clattered loudly when she tossed it to the plate. "We didn't before, and this time we'll put Pierus in his place forever."

"Forever? That didn't work so great with the Titans. How many times have those idiots been freed from limbo?" Clio gripped the paper tightly between numb fingers. "Polly, what do you know about The Five Nations?"

"It's an Eastern European collective. Think the European Union but based on a military mission. They've been in the news lately for some questionable practices. Anything they can do to exploit the poorer nations near them, they've done. Invasion, genocide, ethnic cleansing." Polly grimaced. "There was some think tank in DC that tried to blow the whistle on their activities months ago." Polly curled her lip. Her look made it apparent the outcome hadn't been entirely successful. "When the politicians refused to listen to their warnings, a couple of the senior members of the tank up and quit. I can do some digging and see if I can find any of the former employees."

Callie nodded. "Good. Polly, you check current information. Pierus wrote 'once more.' Does he mean history is repeating? Like there's an easy solution mortals missed in the past? Clio, I want you to dig backward. Look into invasions, genocides, and the like. Not just recent ones, but events from ancient history. Go back a couple thousand years. That's where we'll find our answers. We'll figure out who we need to sway to win this time around."

"But the challenge says one Muse, one man. How do we find the one man?" Clio questioned. This was the part that worried her most. "And what if he doesn't want to help?"

Callie shrugged and then cast a glance around the crowded bar, her icy blue-eyed stare skidding over all the men present. She lowered her brows. "According to the message, they'll find us. Our test will be to inspire them to help solve the problem."

"Who's first?" Nia asked in a small voice.

"Pierus specifically mentions history. It must be Clio." Callie looked expectantly across the table.

Holy Hades, she did not want to go first. She did not want to go at all. Clio lifted her hands in the air. "Why me? You're the oldest, Calliope. Why wouldn't he start with you?"

"Hell if I know," Callie snapped. "It isn't my challenge, so I have no way of knowing what the order will be." She softened her tone. "What I do know is we'll all have to work together to win. Just as we did when we defeated the magpies the last time."

Lost in thought, Clio drummed her fingers on the table. The collective of five separate countries had been encroaching on the borders of their much smaller neighbor and was poised for invasion. "What is the biggest threat to humanity posed by The Five Nations' aggression? If they succeeded in their quest, what would be the worst that could happen?"

"Oligarchy or despotism would be unleashed. Communism or Nazism times a billion. Think ethnic cleansing. Anyone who doesn't hold to the same philosophy of the ruling party, or isn't exactly like those in power, would be at risk," Polly replied. "So Tyranny must be the first daughter up. Saving the world from oppression seems a pretty damn good reason to influence one mere mortal to make a difference."

Shoving papers back into her bag, Callie muttered. "Figures we'd have to persuade a man to help with the challenge we're to solve. Pierus always was a chauvinist. Like we can't do it by ourselves."

Clio bit her inner cheek to hold in her scoffing laughter. As a romance author, Callie should have seen the magic in teaming up with the right man.

Callie snapped the messenger bag's closures together with a sharp click. "Clio, you and I should meet with Gaia as soon as possible."

Their mother. Clio's head started pounding, a raucous tempo that attempted to keep up with her heart. After many lifetimes of dealing with her mom, Clio still dreaded the doublespeak and vague references the woman preferred. It seemed like nothing she'd ever done was good enough. Especially when Callie was involved in the interaction. Her oldest sister had always been the favorite. Except for that one instance when Terri, another sister, had inspired Tchaikovsky to compose Swan Lake. Terri had been the preferred child for years after that.

"Clio! Pay attention. Meet me at the Achilleion tomorrow at noon."

As much as she loved the waterfall that had been named for a garden in Corfu, going there to meet with their mother sucked all the joy out of the bubbling, churning spillway. "Callie, that's my lunch hour. It's my only free time all day." Clio squinted as she sent a mental nudge toward Callie, hoping to sway the decree that she be present at a meeting with Gaia.

Callie's return nudge into a corner of Clio's mind stung like a wasp. Damn, she needed to perfect her shielding from the sharpness of her sister's non-verbal pokes. Clio rubbed her temples.

Callie heaved an exasperated sigh. "Don't you freaking try to nudge me. And quit bitching. I'm on a deadline with edits, but if I can make time to save the damn world, then you can, too." Callie rudely pushed Polly out of the booth.

As their sister cleared the way for Callie's exit, Callie pinned Clio with a hard look, her eyes glittering in the dull light of the bar. She pushed a hank of her russet hair behind one ear, leaving the other side to swing freely against her cheek. "Do not be late, sister."

Heads turned in Callie's wake as she swished out of the pub. Her graceful, statuesque frame was the very thing that inspired most men to think with their dicks, not their smarter heads. And Callie knew how to work it. Clio had to blow a kiss at five foot four to get anywhere near the height. She wished she shared the kind of sexual confidence Callie had in droves. Damn, she couldn't believe she was still comparing herself to her sister. Not after all the years of their existence.

Time to address the more practical aspects of the challenge. With a sigh, she surveyed her remaining sisters. "I wonder if the sudden bad weather has anything to do with Pierus's return? Have there been other abrupt climate shifts whenever he crawls out of the grotto? The last two weeks have felt like an ominous portent."

Nia grabbed the pen the waitress had left with their bill. "Good question. I'll check. I don't think we've ever noticed a changed weather pattern before." She scrawled on her forearm. The black ink stood out on her pale skin.

"Nia, why not use a napkin to write yourself a note?" Polly asked, laughter oozing in her question. "Or your phone?"

"I lose napkins. I'm not likely to lose my arm, am I?" Nia's slightly crooked smile illuminated the darkened booth. "Unless I suddenly become the Venus de Milo."

Clio grabbed the pen from Nia. After quickly scribbling her name at the bottom of the charge slip, she dropped the pen and pushed the paper away. "I'm going to the library to start my research. I know just the place to begin."

"But it's after nine. Isn't the building locked down?"

"Being the big cheese has it perks. I have access." Idly she wondered if she'd find Jax there at this time of night. He'd asked her to be his research assistant, but truth was, she could use one of her own right now.

Good thing she was a Muse and could function on little sleep. It looked as if it was going to be a long, lonely night.

Chapter 4

The library's bright portico light above her head turned Clio's fingers into blurs of white as they flew over the keypad. Within seconds of entering her access code, the tiny LED light at the top of the pad flashed from red to green. The wooden door handle was ancient, smooth, and warm as she pulled it open. She slipped inside the vestibule and waited until the door sealed shut again. Before advancing to the front desk, she slicked her hands over her hair to remove the raindrops and, hopefully, contain the curls that appeared without fail on rainy days like this.

"Hey, Clio." Zeke Patterson, the library's head security officer, greeted her. "It's unusual to see you here this time of night."

At one time she'd been a little more than friendly with the man. But they'd lacked the chemistry to make her want to escalate their coffee dates to any kind of real date. However, they'd managed to maintain their friendship, an arrangement Clio valued more.

Her existence was linked to human mortality. She lived and died on a mortal timetable. This was her one-hundred and twenty-seventh mortal lifetime. And from the time women could enroll in college, she had. She loved the chance to influence her classmates.

Since graduating in this incarnation, though, her track record with men had been dismal. This time around, she'd only inspired her senior year boyfriend to cheat on her with a sorority sister instead of proposing marriage, as Clio had been hinting for him to do. She should have known something was off when she had hesitated to use her goddess gift to nudge him harder as Aerie, the Muse of Love, had suggested. Thank the goddess she'd resisted her younger sister's prompts. Otherwise, she'd have ended up married to the jerk. Still, in the end, Clio's heart and her confidence had splintered. She'd held most men at arm's length ever since.

Overhead lights cast shadows on Zeke's ruggedly handsome face and accentuated the red-gold strands in his blond hair. The sound of a baseball game on the iPad on the desk filled the quiet air.

Clio gave him a warm smile as she scanned her badge. "Evening, Zeke. I have some research to do and figured I'd get a start on it."

Zeke reached over to swing the gate open. "No time like the present, right?"

She scooted through the barrier. Pausing beside him, she peeked over his shoulder at the game score. "Hey, we're winning." She snagged a stack of messages from her mail slot and rifled through them. Requests for special editions and cards from appreciative patrons thanking her for her assistance. A phone message from the university president. Really, the man needed to learn to navigate the college's e-mail system.

"We were down by two in the third, but the Demons struck back like their tails were on fire." Zeke tilted the tablet to give Clio a better view. "Where are you going to be working tonight? Want to make sure not to sneak up and scare you on my rounds."

"Appreciate that." He'd been good about making enough noise to wake the dead since the first time he'd materialized in the room where she'd been lost in a project. He'd scared ten years off her life. A drop in the bucket really. "I'll be in the Ancient Civ room."

"Busy room tonight."

Clio glanced at the screen on the computer monitor. Her heart sped up at the sight of Jax's name on the line above hers. "Professor Callahan is there?"

Zeke pointed to his check-in time. "Been up there for a couple of hours."

Anticipation pinged around her belly like a leaf being blown in a breeze. "Well, I better get to it."

"Have fun." His attention back on the game, Zeke waved absently over his shoulder as she departed.

The night lighting at the library was eerie. The chandeliers had been turned off at closing time. Wall sconces created scattered pools of light on the floor and guided her toward the staircase. The marble steps, worn smooth in spots by years of use, were shadowed and spooky. As many times as she'd been here late at night, she never lost the urge to race up the stairs two at a time. Her imagination always conjured goblins or spirits, nipping at her heels as she climbed. She also never lost the compulsion to laugh at her imaginings.

Cresting the stairs to the second floor, she continued to the third, the strap of her backpack clutched between her fingers. Even though she knew exactly who was in the library at the moment, her nerves pinched the base of her scalp, stinging like red-hot needles. The words of Pierus's e-mail seared her mind. And when did a long-dormant demi-god learn about e-mail?

Reaching the third floor, she rounded the balustrade and pressed a hand against her breastbone. Her heart banged against her ribs. Nerves or anticipation? Pausing a moment, she rolled her shoulders, as if that would help her shrug off her anxiety. At the end of the long hall, a puddle of light spilled from the open door of the Ancient Civ room. Good thing she knew Jax occupied the room. Otherwise, she might scurry back down the steps to the safety Zeke represented.

She moved quietly toward the door. As she approached, she noticed the soothing alto tones of a lyre. Before entering, she paused and leaned her back against the wall by the door, listening to the sound that had filled all her childhoods. Was Jax listening to the ancient melodies as inspiration for his research? It was a trick Clio had used to great effect when focusing on a problem. When a rich baritone voice joined the accompaniment, Clio realized he was singing.

Something primal swirled in her belly. Pressing a hand against the butterflies, a smile tugged the corners of her mouth. Words sung in an ancient Greek dialect flowed through the cracks around the partially opened door. She easily translated the lyrics that paid homage to a woman's body, and she wondered if he understood the words or was merely reciting.

Inside the room, a loud *thunk* was followed by a soft curse, again in another nearly forgotten language. Suppressing a chuckle, and not wanting to startle Jax, Clio knocked on the doorframe before she swung into the room.

"Good evening, Professor," she greeted him as she advanced toward the table where he was madly mopping up spilled liquid.

Jax's head flew up sharply, his eyes wide under dark brows. A smile formed on his lips when he caught sight of her.

"Hello." He stopped wiping up his mess, and the spill leeched toward an antique volume lying on the corner of the table.

Clio hurried across the room. She plucked a stack of napkins off the nearby table. Wadding them up, she blotted the brown liquid away. "Jax, you aren't supposed to have drinks in this room."

Dull red seeped into his cheeks. He grabbed the upended to-go cup and joined her in cleaning up his spill. "Sorry, I meant to leave it outside the door. But I did bring extra napkins, just in case." He shoved the soggy mess into the cup then tipped it toward her. She crammed the wet papers into the opening.

While he threw it into the trash bin by the door, Clio moved the texts he'd been working with to another table, just to be safe. The room plunged into silence as soon as he turned off the playback on his phone.

"Hey, I liked that." She beamed a smile his direction. "There aren't any rules against music. Especially if it fits the period of the room you're working in."

Shrugging, Jax restarted the music app. Dulcet tones filled the silence quite nicely. He set the phone down and turned to face her. "Well, it definitely fits this room."

"I heard you singing. Do you actually know ancient Greek or do you just have the words memorized?" She fussed with the corners of the stack of books, aligning them as she leaned one hip against the table.

"I...um, I'm proficient in several 'lost' languages. Mycenaean Greek is just one of them." He crossed the small space between them in three strides and stopped by her side. "I've loved linguistics since I read my first Tolkien book where he created his own language. It helps with, uh, helped with my last job."

Even though he stood a good foot away from her, heat from his body invaded her space, wrapping her in warmth. She'd forfeit one of her lifetimes to sink into his arms in a real embrace. She strained his direction before common sense beat down her fanciful longings. She needed to get to her research soon or she'd be here all night. But flirting a little while longer wouldn't hurt.

She eased her butt onto the table and swung her legs. "*Helped*? Past tense?"

Nodding, he crossed his arms over his chest. His bulging muscles strained the seams of his tight T-shirt. *Sure didn't look like most of the other faculty professors.* "Yeah. My previous employer required it."

"Did you work for a translation service?" She felt a little like Christopher Robin, trying to pry Winnie the Pooh's nose from the honey jar.

"No."

"Come on, spill it," she encouraged with a grin.

With a barely perceptible lift to his shoulders, he darted his eyes to the side. Her smile apparently trumped his resistance. "I worked for an international think tank. My job was to advise the government how not to repeat past mistakes. Being able to translate ancient accounts of the events leading up to war was key." He blinked his eyes hard and shifted his weight back on his heels.

Clio idly wondered if he'd ever read something she'd inspired. Maybe even one of the ancient texts she'd written herself.

His words penetrated into her wandering thoughts. *Repeat past mistakes.* She stopped swinging her legs and gripped the edge of the table. Could it be this simple? Was Jax the man Pierus had foretold as the one to aid her in this challenge? She nudged again. "What kinds of mistakes?"

Brows raised, he clasped his hands together and spread his legs. "My specialty was in analyzing the build-up behind one country invading another, and the potential impact on the general population from said invasion."

He was talking now. Clio pulled the edge off her mental prodding. "And you traded all that glamour for a job as a history prof. What happened?"

"You don't really want to know this, do you?" A frown creased his brow. She longed to reach out and smooth it away.

Instead, since it was possible the fate of the world depended on her focusing, she stayed on task. "Jax, I'm a librarian. I like to know all kinds of things."

At his mulish expression, she decided it was time for a little nudge. Clio focused her energy and sent him a mental image of him spilling his guts to her. She justified it by telling herself it was like speed dating. Gotta get the information out there fast.

He tipped his head and regarded her, running his gaze like a silk scarf over her body. "In a word, burn-out. I spent way too much oxygen trying to convince the people responsible to listen and take action. They lost interest in hearing what I had to say." He sat on the table next to her.

Curling his fingers around the table edge right beside hers, he did a little nudging of his own, his shoulder to hers. He studied her with his deep amber gaze. "I don't know why I'm telling you this. Typically, I don't talk about my previous occupation."

She smiled brightly at him. "I'm easy to talk to? You want to avoid your research at all costs? Just had to unburden your soul and I'm handy?"

"All those things. But you forgot mesmerizingly beautiful. A cold war spy would want to spill his secrets to you." He dipped his gaze to her mouth.

Licking her lips, she leaned away from him. As much as she wanted him to kiss her, she needed him to finish his story. "They didn't listen so you quit? You just gave up?"

He jumped up and grabbed a book from the stack on the table next to him. His fingers whitened on the heavy leather cover as he opened and closed it, a sign of his agitation. It seemed an eternity before he rolled his head from side to side and answered. "I didn't give up. I just lost the ability to—no, the interest—in asking 'what if.' No matter how hard I tried, I didn't seem able to make a difference. I didn't need the stress." He shrugged and turned away.

His words electrified her. There it was. Confirmation that Jax was the man Pierus's e-mail had foretold. At least, he seemed to be the one who could guide her in the challenge. Now the bad weather made sense. The sudden squall the day they'd met and the increasingly wet weather were portents.

But why would Pierus manipulate the weather? Unless he was leading up to invoking awful storms to aid the Five Nations. A storm of any kind might hamper effort to offer humanitarian aid overseas. It could also lead to power outages here, making her job more difficult. But, would it make that big of a difference to her challenge?

She recalled the day she'd met Jax. During a break in the storm, the sun had peeked through, bathing him in a supernatural bluish glow. Like someone was shining a big spotlight on him.

But how in the name of the goddesses was she supposed to explain this messed up situation to a man who no longer believed in the magic of *what if?*

She straightened her spine and then slipped off the table. By laying a hand on his arm, she drew his gaze back to her. "Jax, you can't stop believing in yourself. It only takes one man to alter the course of history. Unfortunately, it's almost always an evil man. Hitler, Stalin, Napoleon. Even farther back...Attila, Genghis Khan, Alexander. Why shouldn't you be one of the good guys?"

"Don't care about being one of the good guys." Jax stroked his hands from her shoulders to her fingertips and back. His whispery touch and husky voice raised goose bumps on her arms. "I'd like to be your guy."

He lowered his head, hesitating a brief instant before slanting his lips over hers. The warm tender press of his mouth decimated her ability to think. When he curled both hands around her neck and stroked his thumbs along her jaw, a slow, melting sensation claimed her midriff. He changed the angle of his head and deepened the kiss, intensifying the current between them. Clio rested her hands on his biceps, flexing her fingers into the hard muscles playing under his supple skin.

He didn't press any closer to her body, didn't try to close the miniscule gap between his chest and hers. His kiss was oddly friendly, yet steamy. Pulling his mouth from hers, he held her gaze, a smile lurking on his lips. Her stomach did a slow roll at the hungry look in his eyes and her body strained toward his. Threading his fingers through her hair, he reclaimed her mouth. This time, his kiss was deep and slow and drugging.

Rain began pelting the window, rattling it in its frame. A sudden thunderous explosion boomed in the small room, followed quickly by a vibrant flash of light. The scent of ozone filled the room. She jerked backward. The tug on her scalp was painful when Jax didn't immediately relax his grip. "Ouch!" Her eyes watered.

"Oh, God, I'm sorry." Jax stroked his hand on her head, his touch soothing.

"For pulling my hair or for kissing me?" She tangled her fingers with his and pulled their joined hands away from the stinging spot.

"Well, I'm not sorry for kissing you," Jax answered, his tone playful.

Thunder rumbled again, and the lights flickered and dimmed. His fingers tightened on hers as they waited for the power to return to full strength. A flash from the lightning splashed wickedly across the ceiling.

Clio gasped when she spied the form of a man in the block of light coming from the bank of windows on the opposite side of the room. Pierus! Hands raised, palms facing together, his spectral outline vibrated on the ceiling in time with her quivering heart. She tightened her grip on Jax's hand and glanced at the window. Crazy, but she almost expected to see the god hovering outside, three floors up, like something out of a bad horror movie. Nothing.

"You're not afraid of the storm, are you?" he questioned, pulling her hand to his lips and kissing her knuckles.

"No. Maybe." Clio focused her attention on the wall over Jax's shoulder.

Lightning flared again, and this time the shadow included a large, menacing bird sitting on his shoulder.

She whipped around, bouncing off Jax's chest as she did. Bracing her hands on the table, she stared out the glass, waiting for the next flash to see if Pierus was in fact framed in the opening. Maybe he was only visible during the flares. The seconds ticked slowly away. What was taking so long?

Jax steadied her with one warm hand between her shoulder blades, the other on her hip. "Are you okay?"

Bright light illuminated the room again. Nothing appeared outside the window.

Oh, she was afraid, but not of the storm. She feared for the safety of the world if she lost this challenge. The sizzling kiss between her and Jax, coupled with the abrupt reappearance of the storm and the shadow of a megalomaniac with one of his bitchy daughters perched on his shoulder, were proof that her challenge had begun. And Jax was the man destined to help her.

"I'm fine. Just startled is all," she lied.

The lights stabilized in the library, and the storm dissipated. Pierus had made his presence known and, for now, she hoped he'd be content to sit back and watch, waiting for his chance to defeat her and her sisters.

God, it seemed so melodramatic to say the fate of the world rested on her ability to get this charming man, standing protectively at her back, to ask *what if* once again. To envision the magic he could work in the world. But if Tyranny transformed back to goddess form, she wouldn't be satisfied by what was happening in Eastern Europe. Like wildfire, she'd spread her evil ways through each continent.

The lyre music from his phone switched to a cello concerto she recognized from a symphony she'd attended in the eighteenth century. Imagine explaining to him that her sister, Terri, was responsible for Schumann being able to complete his best work in just two weeks.

She glanced at him to find his beautiful eyes filled with

concern. She gave him a slight smile. "We should probably try to work while the lights are on."

"Actually, I was finishing up as you came in. Five minutes later, and I would've been gone."

"Clearly my timing is inspired." Clio laughed.

His warm chuckle wrapped around her heart and cinched in close, leaving her breathless and hot for the man.

"I can stay to help with your project. I'm an excellent research assistant. What are you working on, by the way?"

She sobered. "A student request came in today. She needs, um..." Oh, jeez, she was going to have to think fast for a reason other than the end of the world as they knew it. "She needs information pertaining to architecture and its influence on cinematic expression."

And oh, holy hell, that almost sounded reasonable.

"Well, I can't help you out there. Not my area of expertise." He grasped her hand and tugged her against his chest. "Here is something I'm good at, though..."

He lowered his head and licked along her bottom lip. When she opened in response, he delved inside, stroking his tongue along hers. The sensuous rasp lassoed her belly and pulled her girl parts taut like an invisible, erotic tether. She slid her arms around his shoulders and returned his kiss, lick for lick, nibble for nibble. He gathered her close, near enough to feel his erection through their clothes. Between her legs, heat surged, begging for a full release.

She was panting by the time they broke apart. She nestled her face in his neck. "Okay, yes, you are good at that."

His soft groan teased her ear, his breath stirring her dangly earring. "You aren't half bad yourself.' He leaned away from her, pressing his hips to hers, arms snug around her waist. "Clio, I want to date you. I...I want to more than date you. I've imagined how sweet you'd taste since the moment I met you, and I wasn't wrong. Will you have dinner with me? Right now?"

She stroked her hand along the scratchy stubble on his cheek. "Jax, it's nearly midnight."

"Fine. Then tomorrow. Go out with me tomorrow night." He nipped her lower lip, then soothed the sting with a slow lap of his tongue.

They'd known each other for only two weeks. But that's how long she'd been attracted to him. Plus, he appeared to be the one man Pierus's prophecy foretold. "Okay. Tomorrow."

He released one of his arms and shot his fist into the air as thunder growled again.

She gave him one final mental poke, designed to get him to ask the *what if* question. She should feel guilty the bump included a suggestion he think about her all night long. But she didn't. She wouldn't lie to herself and say she just wanted his help to save the world. Nope, there was no denying she wanted this captivating man to want her.

Oh, yes, the race to the end of the challenge was definitely on.

Chapter 5

J ax hadn't been able to get Clio from his thoughts. Interest in the woman had begun to feel like an obsession. He dreamed of her in his arms, in his bed, on the floor in his living room. The weight of her legs over his shoulders felt real. He'd awoken from that particular early morning fantasy uncomfortably aroused. While he beat off in the shower, he'd imagined her lips on his dick. His hand was a poor substitute for the warm, wet cave he knew her mouth would be.

Even the five-knuckle shuffle hadn't really taken the edge off his need. Despite rubbing one out in the shower, his damned cock remained hard enough to pound nails while he'd shaved and dressed. He drank his coffee, ate a bagel, and read the newspaper standing at the kitchen sink, not wanting the painful constriction that came with sitting on a hard chair with a hard-on.

By the time he'd poured a second cup and scanned the headlines, he had better control of his body. Then he spied a news story about the recent maneuvering of the Five Nations along the border of the much smaller Bulgaria in Eastern Europe. It appeared the coalition comprised of Ukraine, Serbia, Romania, Turkey, and Greece was setting the stage to invade the small monarchy. Reading about it speared a different kind of tension through him. This was exactly the kind of tactic he'd expected and had warned the State Department about. There had been ways to circumvent the build-up, but those in charge had told him to take his advice and fuck off.

Disgusted, he folded the paper and dropped it into the recycle bin by the back door. After pouring himself a to-go mug of his extra strong morning brew, he shut off the coffee pot. He locked the front door behind him. Delphi was a small town, but no sense taking chances.

He turned right out of the gate of the white picket fence surrounding his yard. Last night's nasty weather had cleared. Sun dappled through gaps in the leaves of the large trees lining the residential street. The walk to his office was only fifteen minutes. He pulled the strap of his satchel over his head and adjusted it across his chest. It was going to be hot on the walk home, but for now, his short-sleeved shirt was perfect.

As he jaywalked across the street heading toward campus, a man stepped from behind the large, old oak tree on the corner. The guy waved at Jax. "Good morning, Professor."

"Hello." Jax studied the man's face, but didn't find it familiar. He nodded politely and resumed his march toward campus. The man matched his step to Jax's long stride.

Jax's guard edged up. "I'm sorry, have we met?"

"I haven't had the privilege, but I know who you are. My name is Peter Russell."

Jax continued walking, the unmistakable feeling of being escorted lying uncomfortably along his spine. "Are you employed at DCU?"

Russell's curly hair framed a high forehead. He had a bright blue scarf, the color of the Greek flag, wrapped around his neck, even though it was the middle of summer. He wore rope-soled Jesus sandals with his khaki trousers.

Russell shoved his hands in his pockets and shook his head. He lifted his right brow and said, "Oh, no. I'm simply visiting. I've wanted to meet you for some time now. I'm a fan of your work at GeoPoly."

That brought Jax up short. He stopped abruptly and faced the man. No one but Ian knew about his former employer. Even Clio didn't know the name of the tank. Warning bells clanged like an alarm clock in his mind. "I don't know what you're talking about. I work at the university."

"Now. But your performance with the super-secret think tank has been noted."

Anger built like steam in Jax. "Who the fuck are you?"

A wild screech accompanied the flapping wings of a bird from overhead. Jax hunched up his shoulders and glanced up to see a large black and white bird land on a thick tree branch above the man's head. The bird's repeated call rattled like a machine gun.

"Oh, no one important. I just wanted to ask one question of you. How does it feel to know you weren't persuasive enough to save thousands of lives? If only you'd been able to make them listen. It must be a huge burden to know you could have made a difference." The man leaned his weight on one hip and tipped his head to the opposite side. "Why, the scientist responsible for finding a cure for cancer might have been among the casualties. And his knowledge was lost to the world because you didn't do your job."

Guilt roared through Jax's system like a freight train. Hulking, furious, lava-hot. Jax clenched his fist around the strap of his bag and spread his feet wide, bracing against the blow of Russell's words. "Listen, you shitstain—"

"No, my friend. You must listen." Russell lifted his hand and waved it in front of Jax's face. "You have a great task ahead of you. You will fail. Perhaps, you shouldn't even try."

Pressure built at the crown of Jax's head, as if something—someone—crushed their hands tightly around it. Pain burst behind his eyes, and he squeezed his lids closed. A chuckle rang in his ear, the sound chilling.

"You will fail."

A pop of air blew across his shoulders, and the pain in his head dissipated. The sharp tang of something volcanic, like sulfur, stung Jax's nostrils. When Jax opened his eyes, Russell had vanished.

Looking for the man, Jax spun in a quick circle. It was like he'd never been there. If this was a dream, he'd prefer to go back to the one about Clio. He rubbed his eyes with the heels of his hand. "What the fuck?"

A maniacal cackle sounded overhead. He looked toward the branches and found the bird once again. It tilted its head to the side, studying him. After a couple of rapid blinks of its beady, black eyes, the magpie flared its white striped wings and launched off the limb. Jax ducked as the creature swooped toward him. When it pulled up at the last second and flew away, it lost a feather. The thing drifted down to land on the front of Jax's shirt. He plucked it up, darting his gaze between the departing magpie and the feather.

He shook his head, trying to shed the apprehension that had bloomed in his chest the moment Russell had stepped from behind the tree. "Shitty weather last night, crazy old men, and dive-bombing birds. Not the way I wanted to start my job."

Twirling the feather between his fingers, and with one last glance up and down the street, Jax hustled away.

* * *

Vines and Grecian statues lined the long avenue leading to the Achilleion waterfall. Clio wasn't late, but she could guarantee Callie and their mother would be early. She spared a glance at the statues of her sisters as she hurried past, sticking her tongue out at the statue that depicted Calliope. Childish, yes, but immensely satisfying.

Recent rain had swelled the amount of water churning

down the wide marble steps of the man-made spillway. In a pool at the bottom of the falls a statue of Poseidon, looking commanding and powerful, rode on a pair of seahorses. The God of the Seas didn't actually look anything like the statue. He was small and unassuming and traveled by dolphin. Ever since some renaissance artist had painted her uncle in a chariot behind straining seahorses, the image had stuck.

The spikes of Clio's high-heeled sandals sank into the soft earth as she trotted up to the top of the falls. As expected, she found her mother and sister waiting under a covered picnic area meant to look like a Grecian temple. Clio wiped the sweat from her brow then dried her hands by shoving them into the pockets of the soft cotton dress she wore. As Clio stepped onto the marble floor of the structure, her mother studied her, Gaia's normally smooth forehead wrinkled by a frown.

"Good afternoon, child." Gaia's voice sounded like delicate wind chimes. She tilted her chin up, offering a cheek for Clio's kiss.

"Mother," Clio greeted her. She bent and pressed her lips onto her mother's satiny skin. Gaia wore a floaty sundress that draped her form the way togas had back in the third century. She also had arranged her curly hair in a similar style, gathered on the crown of her head and curling loosely down her back. A yellow ribbon, the same shade as in her dress, was woven like a snare around the top half of the ponytail.

Nodding to Callie, Clio backed up until she rested against one of the limestone pillars supporting the faux-painted wooden roof. In the past, she'd found when she'd dealt with these two, she thought better if she remained on her feet.

Callie wasted no time getting to the point. "What did you dig up in your research yesterday?"

"I found nothing useful in the texts at the library."

"Damn!" Callie didn't even try to disguise her frustration.

"Calliope, mind your language." Gaia had never tolerated the coarse language all nine of them had begun using in the last two centuries.

Callie mumbled, "Sorry."

Clio lifted her hand to tuck a strand of hair behind her ear, effectively hiding her smile at their mother's chastisement of the favored child.

Callie held Gaia's eye. "Mother, if we don't find something to guide us, our cause is lost."

Crossing her arms over her chest, Clio cleared her throat. "I said I didn't find anything in the books. But I did find something…someone to help us."

"Really?" Her mother's speculative gaze remained steady. A slight smile played on her lips.

How was it that her mother always seemed to know what was happening in Clio's life? Like Mother Nature, the woman couldn't be fooled.

Callie didn't show the same restraint. "What do you mean…someone?"

Clio hesitated. Once she mentioned Jax's name, he'd be inexorably tied to the challenge. If she didn't reveal what had happened between them, the hot-as-hell kiss, the sudden thunderstorms, the shadows displayed on the ceiling in the flashes of lightning, she could keep Jax out of it. And safe. The instant she shared what had occurred in the two weeks since she'd met him, he became part of the whole mess.

Gaia dipped her chin and raised her brows. Her eyes commanded, without saying a word, Clio to spill her guts. The nudge pinched painfully on the tender curve of flesh where Clio's neck met her shoulder.

Goddess, she hated when her mother or sisters jabbed her. There weren't any rules saying they couldn't hit each other mentally. But personally, she liked to avoid the stinging jolts when she could. Immortal to immortal nudges felt different than when she sent inspiration to a mortal. The mortals felt like an idea had sparked, accompanied by a typical adrenaline rush.

"Ow! Mother, stop." Clio flexed her fingers on the spot Gaia had targeted and soothed the sting with a mental rub of her own. "I believe I've already met my guide for the challenge."

Callie jumped up and demanded, "Who? Where?" She jammed her hands on her hips and tapped her toe impatiently.

"Two weeks ago, a new history professor, Jax Callahan, joined the DCU faculty. The day we had that awful squall. Remember that?"

"The day I started receiving cryptic e-mails. Before we knew what—who—we were up against." Running her hands through her hair, Callie strode from one side of the shelter to the other. Clio called it Callie's thinking stride. When her sister reached the edge of the cement pad, Clio noticed a couple of black and white feathers that had molted off some bird. The sight of them chilled her.

Callie turned and lifted one brow. "Well?"

Clio pushed the sense of foreboding away. She continued, knowing she was committing Jax to goddess only knew what. "He was at the library last night when I went there after dinner with you, Callie. We got to talking, and he mentioned his previous employer. His last job was as advisor to an international think tank. His role was to analyze potential troop buildup and apply past history to the current situations to try to circumvent possible invasions. And all the evil that comes with marauding armies. Kind of like what The Five Nations Block is doing right now."

Jerking to a stop behind the bench where Gaia sat, Callie clutched her fingers around the top slat and peered at Clio. "It fits."

Gaia patted Callie's hand and posed a question to Clio. "What has you convinced this Jax is meant to be your guide for this challenge, daughter?"

"He told me he'd quit his job because he couldn't make them listen. He got to a point where he no longer believed in the *what if* scenarios." Clio took a seat facing Gaia.

When Callie took up pacing again, Clio tracked her back-and-forth progress. She wished Callie weren't such a perpetual motion machine. It made her nervous.

"Daughter, there is something you are not telling us." Mother squinted as though she was getting ready to poke Clio again.

Clio held her hand up, palm out. "He kissed me. Well, we kissed. It was mutual. And in the midst of it, there was an especially violent burst of thunder. During a particularly long lightning flash, I saw Pierus's shadow on the wall, one of his skanky magpie daughters perched on his shoulder."

"You kissed him?" Callie screeched.

Gaia narrowed her eyes in Callie's direction, who responded by immediately sitting down, rubbing her ear. Good, Clio wasn't the only one Gaia tweaked with her mind.

"Well, this is indeed interesting." Gaia clasped her hands demurely in her lap. "Pierus's message did say you'd have to lead your guide back to magic to enlist his aid in solving the challenge. But why would he deliberately put the man in your path?"

"Did Pierus do it? Is it possible meeting Jax was preordained?"

"You mean like destiny?" Callie scoffed. Sheesh, her sister was awfully jaded for a romance writer.

With a flick of her hands, Clio shooed away Callie's comment. "Maybe Jax believes there is no way we can succeed. Or…Gaia, is there any way his hands are tied by the terms of the challenge?"

Even on Olympus, there were laws governing the way business was conducted. Any activity, business, or challenge was subject to scrutiny and potential sanctions. Including banishment from the pantheon. Or worse. And once a challenge had been issued to a specific deity, all others were limited in the assistance they could provide. To break the rules would be similar to cheating, and not tolerated.

Pierus had violated those rules in his first challenge to the Muses; his cheating had led to Zeus transforming the god's daughters into magpies. It had also set up a vendetta for the ages. Like a bad penny, Pierus kept popping up. Each time, the challenges became more aggressive. This time, Clio believed it more personal toward Zeus. Like the Muses were just a means to an end.

Although the initial e-mail didn't mention it, Clio had to wonder if Pierus had an ulterior motive. Maybe he had a bigger target in his sights than just the Muses.

Insides quaking, she voiced the frightening possibility. "What if he also wants Zeus's crown? With the havoc his offspring could unleash, he could easily pull off a coup—a hostile take over."

Frowning, Gaia mulled over the question. "That's an interesting thought, daughter. I must discuss this with your father."

"Mother," Callie spoke. "How should we proceed with this Jax?"

"Not we, Callie. This is Clio's challenge. It is she who must bring Jax back to the magic." Gaia reached over and patted Clio's knee. "We can help in minor ways, daughter, but you alone must proceed as you deem fit. What do you think should be your next step?"

"I'm having dinner with him tonight. Maybe something will come up in conversation." Uncertainty claimed a corner of her brain. "Should I tell him about me being a Muse? About the challenge we all face?"

Gaia rose gracefully from the bench. She stroked her hand along Clio's cheek, her fingertips gliding smoothly over Clio's skin. "That is up to you, daughter. On this question, all I can say is trust your instincts."

Chapter 6

After the meeting with her mother, which had gone better than she'd anticipated, Clio tried to focus on her work for the balance of the afternoon. Tried, but failed.

She'd shelved an entire rack of books about Renaissance painters in the legal section before one of the student assistants pointed out her error. Together they pulled all the texts and relocated them to their correct home.

With only an hour left in her shift, Clio ducked into the Ancient Civ room to tidy it. Two walls were lined floor to ceiling with bookcases. On the third wall, a half bookcase rested below a bank of windows. A counter ran the length of the fourth wall, with locking cabinets below. The glass display cases above were filled with relics of years gone by. Tools, vases, and tablets depicted a life she remembered from long ago.

After dusting the cases and removing fingerprint smudges from the glass, Clio picked up a stack of books Jax had left on the table. Holding the antique tomes he'd worked with last night, she felt remarkably close to him. She relived their steamy, passionate kiss as she hugged the last volume to her body. Desire bobbed in her chest like a buoy tossed by a wave. Except for the fact he'd lost his ability to believe in magic, he seemed a solid, smart man.

His incredible body held a lot of appeal as well. It didn't take much to imagine how amazing it would feel to be sandwiched between his hard chest and a soft mattress. Tiny zings sizzled under her skin.

Goddess, she wasn't the type to just fall into bed on a first date, but if Jax asked, she'd surrender.

Heat climbed from her belly into her cheeks and stayed there her entire walk home. At least she could blame the temperature for the bright spots of color in her cheeks. Although rain was now out of the forecast, humidity had turned the world into a steamy sauna.

Clio pulled a pretty green and black sundress from her closet. Standing in front of the mirror she held it against her body. The feminine dress made her feel like a Russian princess attending the Czar's court for the first time. The color flattered her red hair and lit a glow under her pale skin. The way the dress was cut, she could go braless and not worry. Something she fully intended to do tonight.

Standing in front of the mirror, she freshened her make-up. So much easier to do now than in ancient Egypt. She shuddered thinking about the kohl and crocodile dung she'd used back then.

Her hand shook while outlining her eyes. She'd blame that on her racing heart. And she'd blame her racing heart on the challenge she faced, not on the idea that Jax might find her desirable.

Tossing the tube of mascara onto the bathroom counter, she sighed at the state of her hair. The moisture in the air had converted her normally sleek style into a riot of curls. A quick glance at the tiny clock by the sink confirmed there was no way in hell she'd have time to straighten the corkscrews surrounding her face. She grabbed her shoes and hurried toward the front room of her comfortable home.

When the doorbell rang, her pulse surged, beating a fast rhythm through her veins. Her palms dampened, so she swiped them against the fabric of her dress before she swung open the door.

Jax stood on her front porch—weight leaned on one hip, looking more handsome than she remembered. His yellow shirt accentuated the amber shade of his eyes and complemented his swarthy complexion to perfection. A black belt circled the waist of his navy blue shorts. The fabric hugged his hips and fell to the top of his knees. Dark hair covered well-muscled calves. He wore flip-flops, and oh, heavens…his feet looked good in them.

While she checked him out, he swept a saucy gaze over her body, a sexy smile adorning his lips. "Hi, gorgeous."

His words lit a flame inside her and spread warmth to her very fingertips. Curbing the urge to fan herself, she stepped to the side and swept her arm in front of her. "I'm almost ready. Come in."

As he passed, she caught a whiff of spice and wood smoke. Goddess, he even smelled good. She skirted around him and led him to her living room where she'd dropped her sandals by the couch. She took a seat to slip them on.

"I'm sorry if I'm early," Jax commented. "I'm always early when I'm excited to get somewhere."

"It's okay." Clio sent him a smile. He could have shown up an hour before the appointed time, and she wouldn't have cared.

He prowled around the room. Near a chair in the corner, he stopped suddenly. "Holy shit!" He squatted, the legs of his shorts rising to expose powerful thighs. Hovering a hand over the instrument, he glanced at her. "May I?"

She nodded. Sweet music filled the air when he stroked his fingers over the strings of her lyre.

When he looked back over his shoulder at her, his eyes had crinkled at the corner and his lips were parted in an appealing smile. "Is this real? Do you play?"

She shrugged her shoulders. "It's real, and I play a little." Standing, she smoothed her dress over her hips before crossing the room to his side.

"This is really old. It looks so authentic." Jax stroked his fingers tenderly over the bell-shaped curves of the instrument.

Clio was shocked by the envy rising in her stomach. She wanted his fingers stroking her as tenderly. Lovingly.

"I found it in a small shop when I visited Corfu." He didn't need to know her travel had taken place over three hundred years ago. "It was bargain priced. I had to have it."

He stood and faced her. "I'd love to hear you play."

"Actually, you really wouldn't. I am a horrible musician. My sister, Terri, is the one you should hear play. The girl is so talented it kind of puts the rest of us to shame."

Cracking a grin, Jax replied, "We all have our special skills." He trailed his fingers down her arm.

Goosebumps rose in the wake of his hand, and her breath shortened. The pulse in the hollow of her neck thrummed. It didn't take much to imagine what his special skill was. "I'm ready."

He trained his gaze on her lips. "Me, too."

Cupping her cheek, he leaned in to take her mouth with his. The kiss was soft and sweet, consuming her with his restrained passion. For such a simple kiss, it created a seismic shift in her chest.

The soft whisper of his breath caressed her lips as he pulled away. When he dropped his hand from her face, she immediately missed the warmth. And when he tucked her hand into the crook of his elbow, she found his action endearing. Jax led her to the front door, pausing long enough to let her snatch her purse from the console table in the hall entryway.

"Where are we going for dinner?" she asked as she locked up her house.

"I'm new in town and, so far, I've only eaten at a bar with a friend or grabbed takeout. My grad assistant told me about an Italian place in University Square—The Copa. Said they have the best food and atmosphere."

"Oh, I love that place." The chef stuck to his ancestors' tried-and-true recipes. The food was definitely authentic.

"Is it walking distance? It's a nice evening." Jax held his hand up, palm facing the heavens, and smiled. "It's not raining. Would you mind?"

"On foot it's about ten minutes away. I'd mind more if you told me you wanted to drive." She laughed. "I love the smell of summer here. Can't get that in a closed-up car."

Jax cast a glance at the three-inch heels of her sandals. "Do you need to change shoes?"

"I'm okay. I walk in heels all the time."

She tugged him down the front path to the street, then steered him to the right. He matched his stride to hers, which she appreciated. Since most men towered over her, she frequently found herself struggling to keep pace. With Jax close to a foot taller, she might have had to jog to stay even.

"How was your day?" he asked as they strolled under the canopy of trees lining the street.

"Busy. It was intake day at the library. We received a new shipment of material for our antiquities rooms. Everything had to be cataloged and tagged." It was detailed work that required concentration. Something she'd lacked today. "How was yours?"

"It started off a little rocky, but improved the instant I knocked on your door."

That might be the nicest thing she'd heard any man say in a long time. Happiness suffused her chest, and she couldn't contain the smile begging for release. He smiled back at her, tightening his fingers around hers.

"I'm sorry it started bad. But I'm glad it's gotten better." Clio swung their joined hands a little higher. "What happened to make it not so great this morning?"

"I had a run-in with some crazy, old bastard and a bird

on my way to work this morning." He shook his head. "The dude told me I had a great task ahead of me. Proclaimed it like an oracle on high. Then told me I'd fail."

Clio stumbled and would have fallen if Jax hadn't thrown his arm across her chest to steady her. Scorching dread burst in her chest and shortened her breath.

"Easy there. Maybe walking in heels wasn't a good idea." Jax wrapped his hand around her arm.

"I'm fine." Had Pierus contacted Jax directly? "And you didn't know the man?"

"Never seen him before." He took her elbow and resumed walking. "But he seemed to know me. He knew the name of my former employer. And some other stuff." Jax's shoulders hunched up as they walked along.

Needing time to process what he'd said, what Jax's meeting with the old man implied, Clio changed the subject to music. She'd definitely learned to multitask over the years.

They turned a corner and entered the square. Pressure increased in her ears as they crossed the cobbled plaza. Clio's senses buzzed as she scanned the crowd. Something—someone—supernatural was near.

Nothing seemed out of order or even the slightest bit threatening. People milled around the large central fountain. A statue of Aphrodite poured water from an oversized vessel into the pool, while jets of water rose three feet from the surface. A street musician, his curly hair flopping over his brow, played guitar for the crowd. A large case lay open at his feet. Jax tossed in a couple of bucks as they passed.

She shooed away the sudden case of nerves when they arrived at their destination. As Jax reached around her to open the door, she caught his distinctive scent once again. She drew a deep breath and held it, relishing the fragrance.

The maître d' led them to an intimate table for two in front of a window. Clio waited until after they'd placed their orders to broach the subject of the challenge. Her mother had told her to trust her instincts, but that was easier said than done. Since she still wasn't sure how much information to reveal, she opted to wing it based on his responses.

"Jax, do you believe in destiny?"

"Do you mean like, were we supposed to meet?" He stirred a packet of sugar into his iced tea. "I don't know. Destiny isn't very scientific. It can't be quantified or measured. Even in history, you can't really point to instances where the outcome seemed predestined. There are too many contributing factors to each scenario." He tapped his spoon against the glass. A drop of moisture fell to the linen tablecloth as he laid the utensil aside.

Clio stared at the bird-shaped splotch. Was this an omen that she was meant to tell him about the challenge? Maybe, if she stretched her imagination enough. She glanced out the window. Low hanging clouds gathered over the building that housed the history department. The very location of Jax's office.

The musician across the square looked up, their glances crashing together. His eyes flashed blue flame, burning and intense. Even though it had been a century since the Muses' last run-in with the deity, Pierus was recognizable—very little had changed about him from the last time he'd tried to free his daughters from their existence as magpies. Pierus was in a disguise designed to let him blend into the crowd. Clio sat straighter in her seat, fear twisting into a knot in her stomach. Why had he appeared to her now? Was the challenge progressing faster than she thought?

She dragged her attention from outside and focused on Jax. "What if I said I'm supposed to help you accomplish this great task you're supposed to undertake? The one the old man mentioned this morning?"

Skepticism etched itself in the way Jax lowered his

brows. "Clio, that man was demented. The only great task ahead of me is learning my students' names and getting them to work up an interest in the political history of the world."

Clio pursed her lips together as the waiter delivered their salads and a plate of bread. What seemed an eternity passed while she waited for the server to pour olive oil in a small dish then add seasonings and balsamic vinegar. In fact, it took less than thirty seconds. When he finally departed, she shoved her tomato and mozzarella plate to the side. "I don't think your guy was crazy."

Jax paused, a forkful of lettuce halfway to his mouth. He lifted his brows. "Not my guy. And besides, you didn't see him. Or hear him. He was definitely out of his mind."

"You said he mentioned your former boss. How would he know anything about who you worked for in the past?"

The corners of Jax's mouth turned down. "Good guess? The university sent out a press release when I signed my contract. Maybe he saw a story printed in the paper."

Clio wanted to kiss the frown from his lips. Instead, she pulled the plate toward her and then speared a tomato onto her fork. "Nope, not buying it. Jax, I believe you were meant to run into that man. I think he crossed your path to set off a chain of events that only you can stop."

Releasing a huffy breath, Jax leaned back. "Clio, that just can't be. I've already demonstrated I can't stop anything. It's why my former employer is *former*." Shadows flitted through his eyes.

"Why did you leave?" She kept her voice gentle, sensing it wasn't an easy topic for him.

Training his gaze out the window, he clenched his jaw, making the muscle pop. The longest moment passed before he answered. "I made a bad recommendation. My employer listened. As a result, people died. A lot of people." His tone was gritty and strained, matter of fact.

As if the cost of the words was too high.

Placing her hand over his on the table, she looked deep into his eyes and brushed his mind with a suggestion to let go of the past. To believe he could make a difference. To believe in her.

His brows creased in the middle, and he put a hand to his temple. He shifted in his chair, leaning forward. The shadows in his gaze transformed into something hot.

Before she could continue her effort to convince him, the waiter appeared with their main courses. She moved her hands to her lap. Clio had lost her appetite and could do little more than stare at her plate of pasta and cream sauce. She didn't want to go full disclosure with him. Not yet. Goddess, if he thought Pierus was crazy, he was going to find her certifiable.

"Okay, back to your original hypothetical question," Jax said as he cut a piece of his chicken spiedini. "Let's say I have this magical ability to change the fate of the world. What am I supposed to do? How do I recognize what I'm destined to stop? I'm not in the political world anymore. Now, I simply teach about what happened in the past."

"Can't past history be a predictor of future events? All we have to do is study current events then search the past for similar situations." She drew a deep breath, dug deep for the voice of reason, and forged on. "Like The Five Nations Block. Look at what they're doing. Has anything like it happened in all of recorded time? I can think of a few instances where countries invaded their weaker neighbors with disastrous results."

"How would comparing those events to what's going on now help solve the problem? My whole job with GeoPoly revolved around those exact scenarios of past events as predictors. Politicians are too busy posturing or campaigning. They've stopped listening." Jax reached for his drink, his knuckles white as he gripped the sweating glass.

"Would they listen if you pointed out times when the

invasions were stopped with diplomatic intervention?"

"Not bloody likely." Jax's words were jaded, his tone despairing. "Listen, this is getting to be a downer of a conversation. Can we change the subject?"

"Jax—"

"Please? Let's talk about something a little more pleasant."

Clio bit the inside of her cheek, forcing back the argument begging for release. Distress burned hot in her chest. For his dismissal of the potential problem, for not being willing to at least consider how he might help circumvent world-wide calamity. She reined in the desire to pound the table and make him listen.

She turned her attention out the window. Pierus had vanished. She breathed a little easier for having him gone. There would be opportunity to pursue this further with Jax. Time to get him on her side of the challenge. She hoped.

The rest of the meal passed easily, talk about the university community, the town of Delphi, and the surrounding country. Clio declined dessert, and Jax signaled for the check.

Escorting her from the building, he pressed his palm to the skin bared by her backless sundress. The warmth of his hand built bubbling anticipation under her flesh and in her belly. She looked forward to his goodnight kiss at her door. And maybe, possibly, a good morning kiss tomorrow. She'd definitely welcome him to her bed. Hope dominated her attitude, and she prayed this attraction between them was real and not simply manufactured by Pierus for the sake of the challenge.

In the time they'd been indoors at the restaurant, steel gray clouds had covered the summer sky. Warm wind gusted around Clio's legs as they walked, lifting her dress and fluttering in her hair. They were still five minutes from her house when the first, fat drops splatted on the ground.

One struck Clio on the cheek. She reached up to brush

it away, and another landed on her forehead. "We better hurry. The sky seems ready to pour down on us."

"Weather sure is weird here in Delphi. It was a perfect night when we walked to the restaurant." He flinched when a drop hit his eyelid.

"Hang on." Clio pulled her hand from his. Rain fell more steadily now, and there was no way in hell she'd run in heels. Drops splashed on her bared back as she bent over to slip off the straps of her sandals. She shucked her shoes, the cement warm and rough under her toes. Dangling them from her fingers, she sent Jax a smile. "Now I'm ready. Just in case."

The heavens opened, and water streamed over them. Laughing, they took off running toward Clio's street. By the time they rounded the corner, they were drenched. The folds of her dress clung to her legs, making running difficult. She slowed her pace, plucking at the wet fabric.

Jax pulled her to an abrupt halt. When he wrapped an arm around her back, the other behind her thighs, and lifted her from her feet, she squealed. His smile broadened as he resumed running, bouncing her against his chest.

"Almost home. Got a key ready?" Water ran in rivulets down his face. Glittering drops gathered on the tips of his long, dark eyelashes.

Clio released her grip around his neck to dig through her purse for her house key. Holding her tighter against his chest, he sprinted down the sidewalk.

He pounded up the path to her front door and skidded to an unstable halt, slipping on the steps to the front door. Her laughter rang out over the pelting noise of rain slapping the leaves in the trees.

Once in the shelter of the awning above the stoop, he released the arm under her knees, letting her slide along his body to regain her feet. Water did attract electricity. Hot currents sped along her nerve endings as her damp skin connected with his. His fingers were wet and warm on her back.

Thunder boomed in the distance, drowning out the noise of rain that pummeled the metal awning overhead. Clio jabbed her key into the lock and, a second later, had the door open. Hurrying, she crossed the threshold with Jax crowding in behind.

Chapter 7

T he breath caught in Clio's throat when she turned and her breasts brushed his chest. Searing temptation followed the brief touch. She took a hasty step backward. The coarse wool of the antique rug in the entry hall under her bare feet was the only thing keeping her from melting. Water dripped on the floor from the hem of her soaked dress. The rain had rendered her clothes nearly transparent. Jax's yellow shirt was plastered to his body, defining heavy pectorals and sharply ridged muscles on his abdomen. *Nope, not like any other man on the faculty.* She'd never wanted to lick any other professors.

Holding her gaze, Jax sluiced water from his face. When he wiped his hands on his shorts, her gaze tracked the motion. A thick bulge strained his zipper.

Her nipples drew taut beneath the damp fabric across her chest. No way in hell could she dismiss her physical reaction as a result of the blast of cool air coming from the floor vent behind her.

Jax lunged toward her. Wrapping his arms around her back, he hauled her up against his body. When he bent and trapped her mouth under his, the spark she'd grown accustomed to from his touch erupted into flames. He prodded his tongue past her lips and tangled it with hers. She sucked him deep inside, swirling her tongue around his.

Spearing her fingers into his damp hair, she stretched

up on her toes and dragged his head closer. When her breasts flattened against hard muscles, desire sizzled from the point of contact and pooled low and hot in her center. His kiss turned voracious, his lips devouring her, swallowing her quiet moan. Oh, heavens, this man kissed like a god.

When he groaned, the deep, gruff noise vibrated in her chest as well. His fingertips scorched her flesh as he dragged them down her spine. As soon as he reached the small of her back, he splayed his hands over her butt and pulled her hard against his hips. She gasped when he circled his pelvis, grinding suggestively against her.

"Want you now," he growled against her lips.

With a deft move, he spun them until her body was sandwiched between the hard wood of the door and the immovable wall of his torso. He finally released her mouth and started a sweet, tortuous descent along the column of her neck. He tangled his hand in her hair and eased her head to the side, creating a better angle for his mouth.

She shivered when he licked the hollow between her ear and her jaw. The firm pressure of his hand shocked her when he found her breast. Melting heat rushed between her legs, and sheer pleasure wreaked havoc on her body. The shivers continued as he nibbled his way down her neck. She clutched his head between her hands, flexing her fingers on his scalp. The thumping of her heart matched the sharp staccato beat resonating from his chest.

"Clio...oh, God. Feel what you do to me," he mumbled against the curve where her neck met her shoulder. He thrust his hips against hers and bit hard, then licked and kissed away the sting. "I've never wanted anyone this desperately."

The firm weight of his shaft pressed deliciously into her belly. She lowered her hands to his shoulders and pushed. He stumbled backward, a look of confusion in his eyes. The magnificence of his body stunned her. Broad shoulders tapered to a lean torso and narrow waist and hips. The front of his shorts was stretched taut. The sight of the wide, long ridge dried her mouth and stilled the breath in her lungs.

"I could say the same." Again, she pushed his chest, backing him up a few more steps. She followed. She laid her hands on his shoulders, went up on her toes, and pressed her mouth to the corner of his. The skin of his generous bottom lip was satin smooth when she licked. She pushed again and chased after him.

His lips curved into a smile. Catching on to her game, he grasped her waist and voluntarily eased backward. "Where are we going?" he asked between earth-shattering draws on her mouth.

Clio slid her arms around his waist. She wrapped her fingers in his shirt and worked it free of his pants. His skin was smooth and hot when she flattened her palms on his bared back. "Not too far. Just to the end of the hall. I have a nice, big bed for us to roll around on."

Giddy delight rose up her spine when he found the dress's zipper low on her back and eased it down. He dipped his fingers into the opening and rasped his nails gently along her backbone in the wake of the parting material.

Still walking backward, still possessing her lips, he worked the zipper past the curve of her butt. When he dug his fingers into her hips, he groaned again. Finally, he tore his mouth from her. Resting his forehead against hers, his breath rushed in her face. "Your skin is like silk, your lips like roses. God, what you do to me."

Following the urge to be bold, Clio lowered her hand to his shorts. She traced her fingers along the front and then cupped him, eliciting his sharp gasp. Head thrown back, he jutted his hips forward, seating himself more fully in her hand. She massaged the length of him while raining kisses along the rough stubble exposed on the underside of his jaw.

Growling, he grabbed her wrist and pulled her hand around his hip, resting it on the flat of his back. "No more teasing. You keep touching me like that, I'm going to blow. I'd much rather be in you when that happens." His rumbling voice raised goose bumps on her body.

"Me, too."

Weaving his arms around her torso he brought her close against him. When he lifted, she wrapped her legs around his waist. She squeaked when he spun around and banged into the wall. "Sorry, wrong direction. Which way?"

Hooking a thumb backward over her shoulder, she directed him down the hall to the bedroom.

"We need to lose these clothes, Jax."

The hungry smile on his face changed to wicked in the blink of an eye. "Damn straight."

Thanks to the rain, her room was shrouded in gloom. The small lamp she'd left lit on the bedside table cast a warm pool of light over the pile of pillows scattered at the top of the bed.

Jax lifted his knee to the bed between her legs. Her clit zinged as she rode his hard thigh on her way to the mattress. Amazing sensation rose in waves when he slid his hands along her legs. The tide surged when he slipped them under the hem of her dress. Dropping his foot back to the floor, he trailed his fingers along her inner thigh and continued upward. She tilted her hips. There was no stopping her whimpers when he brushed her panties, prodding one fingertip into her slit. If his finger felt this wonderful through the thin lace, having no barrier between them was going to border on explosive.

Jax bent and nuzzled the back of her knee, his lips tickling. He nudged her leg up until one foot rested on his shoulder. He twisted his fingers in the elastic of her bikini panties and tugged. When she lifted her butt, her heel dug into the hollow above his collarbone. Turning his head, he bit her ankle, the pain-pleasure climbing her leg.

Seconds later, he jerked the lacey undergarment down her legs and over her feet. He tossed the scrap of fabric to the floor with a grin. "Now we're getting somewhere. Come here." With a chuckle, he planted his big hands behind her knees. He yanked her to the edge of the bed, arranging her legs on each side of his hips.

Wanting to free him from his clothes, she reached for his belt buckle.

Grasping her wrist, he stilled her motion. "Not yet. I have plans." The stroke of his hand between her legs made her sigh. Another one of his sexy, low chuckles filled the room.

Her nerve endings danced like wind chimes. A soft moan escaped her lips when he pressed one hand on her belly and worked the other under her hips. He went to his knees next to the bed. A second later, his hot tongue caressed her skin as he slowly moved up her leg.

Breath whimpered out of her. She was not above begging. "Jax, please get there soon. Please." Pushing up on her elbows, she watched him leisurely nuzzle his way up her leg.

He lifted the skirt of her dress above her hips, baring her to his gaze. And dear heavens, he took his time staring at her. Outside, thunder boomed, matching the storm building within her with each brush of his fingers, each touch of his lips or tongue.

"You're gorgeous." He licked her. "Rosy and wet"—another lick—"and hot." He sucked her clit into his mouth and dipped a finger inside her. Fisting her hands in the comforter she bit her lips to keep from crying out her pleasure.

A shock of sensation blasted up her belly and lodged under her heart like one of Cupid's arrows. His name was a sigh on her lips. Finding the top of her dress confining, Clio released her grip on the covers and reached behind her neck. She pulled at the ties holding the halter-top in place. The damp ties resisted, then finally gave when she jerked. She lowered the soaked fabric, baring her breasts. Pressing the mounds together, she circled her fingertips on her nipples. Although her hands were smaller than Jax's, she could pretend it was him…kneading her, cupping her. The heat Jax's mouth generated on her slit clashed with the cool air on her chest, pushing her along with the tide.

"I knew you'd taste like cinnamon." He lifted her hips higher, angling her for better access.

He took his time, working magic on her body. Tongue replaced fingers. With each thrust and lick, the wet, slurping noises he made drew her closer to the edge. Each time he nibbled on her clit, or brushed his thumb over the sensitive spot, shards of light and energy sent her farther into a euphoric stratosphere. She lowered one hand to his head and speared her fingers into his short hair, fisting it to draw him closer. He grunted when she pulled but didn't stop moving his mouth on her.

Tension built in her belly and in her chest. Her legs trembled, and she whimpered and begged. A jumble of colors flickered behind her eyelids. She threw her head back as waves of her orgasm crested then crashed over her. She floated on a cloud of emotion…a miracle of passion. Her body quivered as Jax stayed between her thighs, nibbling and licking. Each time he dipped his tongue back inside her, desire trembled anew.

Easing his grip on her hips, he lowered her to the mattress as she panted softly. He held onto her ankles, keeping her feet on his shoulders as he kissed one thigh, then the other before sitting back on his heels.

Summoning energy from deep within, she lifted her head from the bed. Her foot twitched when he stroked his fingers over the curve of her instep. His eyes were hot as he gazed up the plane of her body. Moisture, droplets of her come, glistened on his mouth. When he swirled his tongue over his lips, lapping up every last bit, her entire body clenched. Goddess, she could come again, right this very instant, without one of his fingers inside her.

"Jax, why are you still fully dressed?" She reached for his belt, but her fingertips were numb in a gripping, erotic haze of color and sensation.

"Took care of you first." He slipped her feet from his shoulders. Standing next to the bed, he jerked his buckle open, dragged his shirt from his shorts, and without undoing the buttons, pulled the fabric off. When his head emerged from the opening, his hair was tousled. Her fingers itched to reach out and smooth through it, then continue on down his chest. The ridge behind his zipper was bigger now than when he'd first dropped her to the mattress.

She scooted backward on the bed, her gaze never leaving his body.

* * *

She looked like she could devour him. Which would be abso-freaking-lutely fine with Jax. Dress bunched around her waist, pert breasts bared, legs splayed for his viewing pleasure, damned if she didn't look like Aphrodite, Goddess of Sex. While he'd been worshipping her flesh, he'd glanced up and seen her cupping her own breasts. It was a thing of erotic beauty, reminding him of ancient paintings of Roman orgies.

The memory had blood slamming hard into his throbbing cock, straining against the constricting fabric of his shorts. He was just about goddamned lightheaded from the lack of blood north of his beltline.

The shirt he'd just shed shimmied off his fingers, plopping wetly to the floor. He popped open the button on his shorts. Clio drew her knees higher, opening them wider.

Propped on her elbows, her gaze was locked on his hands. She bit her lower lip.

Stifling a groan, he carefully, slowly began to lower his zipper. She pushed higher onto her hands, her hungry eyes following his motion. He stopped, drew a deep breath, dipped one finger under the elastic of his boxer-briefs, and freed the tip of his dick. Her breasts heaved out on a moan when the dark red head peeked over the edge.

"Jax." The plea in her voice was unmistakable.

"You want more?" He lowered a hand back to his zipper and paused.

Eyes wide and expectant, she nodded. Gorgeous red curls skimmed her jaw with the motion.

He resumed his striptease, each tooth of the zipper clicking as he slowly lowered it. Desire coursed through his veins, and his heart kicked hard in his chest.

The striptease he'd planned to turn Clio on was killing him. All he wanted was to be buried deep within her. To pound into the sweet warmth he'd discovered with his tongue, to lose himself. He finally managed to get the zipper undone. When he lifted his hands to the waist of the shorts, Clio's hand drifted between her legs.

He shot a glance to her face and found a playful smile on her lush lips. His ball sack drew up, the sensation creating tightness at the base of his spine. "Jesus, Clio."

"You're taking too long." She dipped one slender finger into the opening where he wanted to be.

Oh, fuck, the sight of her touching herself was nearly the end of him. He panted and attempted to turn back the surge building inside. Clenching his thighs together, he ordered his dick to stand by. It took everything in him to focus on shoving his pants down. His undershorts quickly followed. Shaft slapping against his belly, he stood before her, ramrod straight.

"Jax, you're…magnificent." Her nostrils flared as she sucked in a breath. She sped up the motion of her finger, her breasts jiggling with each thrust of her hand.

Leaning over her, he grabbed her wrist, stilling her action. "Mine," he growled.

He slipped a finger in next to hers, then swirled them both into motion. When her jaw dropped open, he didn't waste any time slanting his mouth across hers. Greedy, hungry, his tongue mimicked the action of their fingers.

When he pulled back, he held her gaze. He lifted her hand free of her body. Her eyes widened when he licked away the sweet, salty moisture. The tip plopped free of his lips. "This is mine, too."

Dropping her head back, Clio mewled when he slipped his fingers back into her body. Slick, hot. And ready for him.

"Need a condom." He twisted his finger, curling them up to hit her g-spot.

She shuddered. Her eyes were bright when she lifted her head to look at him. "I'm on the pill. And I'm clean."

"Really?"

"Yeah. You?"

"Yeah." His breath stuttered with the idea of sliding his unsheathed dick into her warm, tight pussy. Burning to be in her, his body drew impossibly tight.

"What are you waiting for then?" Clio fisted her hands in his hair and tugged.

Tangling his fingers in the fabric of her dress, he jerked it over her hips and down her thighs, all but throwing it across the room. He climbed onto the bed, then sat back on his heels.

Reaching between her thighs, he plunged his fingers inside twice more before pulling them free. Bracing one hand next to her shoulder, he splayed the other on her stomach and slid up her body. He kissed his way along her collarbone. Stopped to pay attention to her breasts. Cupping one soft, fleshy mound, he pulled the nipple of the other deep into his mouth, twirling his tongue over and around the tight bud.

Clio jerked his hair. "Dammit, Jax. I want you in me now."

The seal between his mouth and her flesh popped softly when he pulled his lips free. He licked the nipple, tugged it with his teeth, then continued upward until he lay atop her. The beaded tips of her breasts seared his chest. The crown of his cock slipped into her pussy. Clio lifted her legs around his waist and locked her ankles behind his hips. Her heels dug into his back, encouraging him to go deeper. God, the urge to pound into her nearly overpowered him. He had wanted a slow, easy loving. But maybe next time.

By sheer dint of will, he stilled the involuntary motion of his hips with just the tip of his dick in her. He slanted his mouth over hers, plunging his tongue inside, stroking over hers. She wrapped her arms around his neck and drew him close, her tongue doing battle with his.

She pulled her mouth free. "Please, Jax. Be in me now." Her voice was a low, needy whisper of emotion against his cheek.

Bracing his arms on either side of her head, he plunged upward to the hilt. Groaning, he rocked his hips forward. Each move inside her sparked his growing need. Her answering gasps only made him drive harder and higher into her. She met each rock of his hips with one of her own. He ground his lower belly into her clit with each thrust and circle.

Her body quivered, and her moans got louder. His name fell from her lips like a carnal blessing, and she begged for more. She arched her back, flattening her chest against his. The walls of her sheath pulsed, milking his cock. Tingles ran from the base of his spine through his body like a sizzling current and drew his sack tight. He dug his toes and knees into the bed, angling for more access, finding a way to plunge deeper.

Just as her orgasm claimed her, jets of hot come burst from him. And kept coming as she convulsed around him, moaning and panting. His heart galloped in his chest like a thoroughbred. Shoving his arms under her back, he grabbed her shoulders and rocked into her again and again. Her breath rushed against his ear as his chest heaved. The heat from her taut nipples seared him as he collapsed onto her.

Moments passed quietly between them. Her muscles continued to clench around his shaft as he lay breathing heavily.

"I wish I could move, but I'm absolutely wrecked," he whispered against her ear.

"You say that like it's a bad thing," Clio teased.

"Am I too heavy?"

She shook her head and locked her legs more tightly around his back in response.

Jax turned his head until his face was buried in the curve of her neck, her body a soft pillow under his. Her chest heaved when she sucked in a deep breath. Dammit, he was too heavy. When he attempted to move, she tightened her arms around his neck to hold him in place. He balanced more to the one side, giving her a slight reprieve from his crushing weight.

While the storm between them had been raging, the storm outside had dissipated to a light rain. The soft plop of water on the windows acompanied their panting breaths.

Above everything else, the incessant cackle of a bird tapped at Jax's consciousness. "That's weird."

"Don't go calling me weird now." God, he loved the low sexy hum of her voice.

He lifted up and balanced on his elbows and looked out the window at the darkened sky. "No, it's weird to hear a bird in the night."

"What about owls? Owls are birds." The skin on her forehead puckered as she squirmed under him and followed his gaze.

When he lifted his hips, she clenched her inner muscles, gripping him like she didn't want to let go. He gasped as he slipped free, then rolled to her side and settled on the mattress. "Birds are typically quiet after the sun goes down. I'm not hearing an owl, more like a raven. Or the bird I saw this morning, a magpie." He laid his hand possessively on her breast and squeezed gently.

Clio stiffened. "A magpie?"

"Yeah, I saw one early today. Messy little suckers, if you ask me. Always dropping feathers and squawking like there's no tomorrow."

Chapter 8

H er world had been sunny in the light of Jax, but it dimmed when he mentioned the bird. Cold dread passed through her like a shadow. Goddess, if she didn't do something, there might not be a tomorrow. At least for her. And as for the rest of civilization, well, all of the possible tomorrows would be vastly changed if she failed. And instead of working toward solving the challenge, she'd fallen into bed with the man whose aid she was supposed to enlist.

She was an idiot.

This was the complete and utter wrong time to try to influence him. Lying naked in his arms, praying he'd make love to her one more time before she had to return to reality. And then a third time. And once more as the sun started its climb on the horizon. She squeezed her eyes together and chewed her lower lip. His soft kneading action on her breast sent waves of desire coursing through her.

Her wants and needs would have to wait. If Jax had seen a magpie, and now heard one outside her window, the challenge must be in full swing. Add in Pierus's appearance as they'd dined, and hellfire, she should be quaking from fear, not need.

Concentrating on Jax's face, she sent him a nudge to get out of bed. But instead, the sexy smile he'd been wearing grew even more incandescent, and he blinked hard. He pressed a kiss to her shoulder and circled the tip of his fingers around her areola.

"We fit together, Clio," he said, his voice soft and seductive.

Jax rested his arm around the top of her head and laid his cheek on his bicep. Toying with her hair, he draped a leg over hers and pressed closer. Against her bare thigh, his dick twitched. The tingling that had never really died flared back to life. Her body was certainly ready for round two. Even if her mind was already elsewhere, like sitting across the room in the chair, away from the temptation of his hands and lips.

Pushing away thoughts of continuing their love play, she firmed her mental jab and sent it toward him again, praying he'd receive the message this time, hoping she wouldn't have to tell him he should leave. Those words, coming from her mouth, had the ability to slay her. Something popped in her chest as she prodded his mind.

He stopped the motion of his fingers on her flesh. Holding her breath, she prayed the stronger nudge worked. The idea to leave her bed had to be his. Because, to be honest, she didn't want him to go. If only Pierus wasn't trying to play a dirty trick that could destroy her sisters and quite possibly the world. She tried to rein in her dramatic thoughts. But knowing if Tyranny were freed from her magpie form, the aggressive position the Five Nations were taking would quickly spread across the rest of the planet. She needed to speak to Gaia.

His cock prodded harder into her thigh. He glided his hand up her chest and throat until he came to rest on her cheek. Urging her face to his, he pressed a kiss to the corner of her mouth. "Forget I mentioned the birds. We have much better things to do than talk."

What the hell was wrong with her? Not one of the prods she'd sent his direction seemed to be effective. He wasn't succumbing to her inspiration. It was as if the stimulation he'd received was different than the message she'd sent. Add one more thing to her list to mention to Gaia.

She broke her silence by releasing an explosive sigh. "Jax, I'm really sorry about this, but we need to talk." Simply saying the words stung her heart. She rolled from his arms and off the side of the mattress, snatching the throw from the bottom of the bed as she did. Regret inched up her chest like someone climbing a ladder. In the blink of an eye, she had the blanket wrapped around her torso. She braced her feet apart on the plush rug.

Jax pushed up on his elbow. His bare chest gleamed in the light from the one small lamp on the bedside table. His black hair was disheveled and one knee was bent upward, the other leg stretched out on her bed. His taut muscles flexed, and the deep vee cut of his lower belly was like a directional beacon to the one part of his body where she shouldn't be looking.

She darted her gaze back to his face, heat charging up her chest and neck. He lay on the bed looking like a marble statue of Hercules, strong, solid...desirable. One eyebrow arched up, and his lips tilted in a crooked smile.

"Did I do something wrong?" he asked, something close to contrition lurking in his tone.

Outside the window, the magpie's call rattled again. Clio clutched the blanket more firmly against her chest and pressed her hand over her eyes. It would be easier to say what she needed to if she couldn't see his chiseled body. If she didn't think about how his muscles moved under her fingertips. "I just... We need to talk." She sucked both lips between her teeth and bit down.

The breath he sighed out sounded resigned. "Okay."

The bed squeaked as Jax climbed out. Clio kept her hand over her eyes, tension blossoming in her neck. His footsteps whispered against the soft rug. The metal of his belt buckle jangled as he scooped up his shorts. She heard him zip his pants and refasten the belt. His footsteps moved away from her.

Dropping her chin, Clio covered her entire face with her hands. A wail built up in her chest that she savagely forced away, along with the thought of how she'd ruined something lovely and magical. She'd lived a long time and couldn't recall ever experiencing what she'd had in bed with Jax.

His steps approached her again. Lowering shaky hands, she snapped her head up. The pale cream-colored robe she'd left hanging on the knob of the dresser dangled from his fingers. She clutched the robe against her chest. Breath stilled in her lungs when he traced the pad of his index finger under her eye, holding her gaze as he did.

Her eyes crossed when he held his fingertip up in front of her face. She was surprised to see moisture glittering like a diamond on the end. She didn't realize she'd shed tears.

He leaned into her, his voice soft when he spoke. "Whatever is wrong, it can't be worth crying about. We can work this out."

His gentle voice shimmered over her skin and settled in her chest, a warm glow just under her heart. She'd known him only two weeks, but already he had this power over her. It didn't take a leap of faith to see they could, in fact, change the path Pierus had cast before her.

With a small tug, Jax took the robe from her hand. "I'll wait for you in the living room." His bare chest brushed against her upper body when he wrapped the garment around her shoulders.

His lips grazed the corner of her mouth, his brown eyes warm and sincere. Everything in her strained toward him, seeking the common sense and calm he offered. With a nod, he moved toward the door. Pausing on the threshold, he glanced back. His attention lighted on the rumpled bed. Lust and longing and something else…contentment perhaps…flickered in his expression.

Sliding his gaze toward her, he sent an encouraging

smile across the distance before exiting.

Clio crossed her arms over her chest and clutched the sides of the robe he'd draped over her shoulders. He moved away with agile grace. When he disappeared around the corner into the front room, she released her pent-up breath in a quiet rush.

If nothing else, with this confident, caring, sexy man at her side, trying to redeem the world might actually be fun. Clio dropped the blanket she'd snuggled around her body and then wiggled into the robe. Before she left the room, she straightened the covers on the bed, smoothed her hand over the indention Jax's head had made on the pillow. She jumped when the magpie in the tree outside her window jabbered—the sound a cold, harsh laughing noise.

Straightening her spine and squaring her shoulders, Clio cinched the belt of her robe tight. She stared into the dark through the window, squinting to locate the damned bird. Not even a vague outline appeared in the branches. Didn't matter. She extended her middle finger toward the window. The gesture was almost as childish as sticking her tongue out at the statue of Calliope at Achilleion earlier. But still, it broke some of the tension consuming her.

Biting her lip against the smile trying to break out, she padded down the hall. What should she say to Jax? How would the story she was about to confide affect him? She rounded the corner into her living room and stopped when she caught sight of him.

He stood framed in the window, his back to the room, one elbow braced on the wall, his hand cupping the back of his neck. The tails of his shirt hung loose around his lean hips, his bare feet shoulder-width apart. The only indication that he was tense came from the set of his shoulders. His forlorn posture stung like a wasp at her heart.

"Jax." She stopped. She still didn't know what to say to him. Goddess knew she wanted to spill the whole truth about herself. The urge had never been so strong, so overwhelming.

He turned. He hadn't bothered to button the shirt, and the edges gaped open, revealing the smooth expanse of his pectorals. Leaning against the windowsill, he rubbed his fist over the center of his chest. He watched her with expectant, wary eyes.

She crossed the room and took a position behind the tall wingback chair by the fireplace. Recognizing it as a defensive posture, she scooted to the side and leaned against the upholstered wing. She scratched her short nails along the padded headrest. Desire to stroke his thoughts, to make him more receptive to what she had to say nearly overrode her determination to do this the mortal way. To be fair to him, she had to keep out of his mind when she asked for his help. Regardless of how much it galled to admit.

His sigh rang in the quiet of the room. "Look, I know we haven't known each other long. But you shouldn't be embarrassed about what just happened. We're adults. We both wanted it. So what if it seems sudden?"

"No! Oh, goddess, Jax. You think I regret my decision to take you to bed? Nothing could be further from the truth. Half of me is kicking the other half for not asking *you* on a date sooner. We're damn good together."

His eyes widened briefly, but then narrowed again. Shaking his head, he let his shoulders slump. "Then what is it?"

"You're not going to believe what I'm about to tell you." Why would he? Gods and goddesses were merely myths in the eyes of the pragmatic world. They didn't exist. *She* didn't exist. She gestured to the sofa. "Take a seat. Can I get you a drink? Beer? Whiskey?" Giving him something strong to drink might make him more comfortable and willing to embrace what she had to tell him. She could use a stiff drink herself.

"Sure." Jax took a seat on the edge of the couch cushion, bent forward, and propped his elbows on his knees.

Clio headed to the small cupboard opposite the fireplace. Crystal glasses were arranged on top, and she dragged two toward her. The amber-colored whiskey in the etched decanter was an exact match to the shade Jax's eyes had darkened to as he'd moved within her a short while ago. As she poured three fingers of the spirit in each glass, several drops of whiskey spilled out when her hand shook.

Drinks in hand, she moved back to the sofa. She took a seat next to him and downed a healthy swig from her glass. The whiskey burned a path straight to her belly. Cold practicality iced a spot in her chest right next to the burning uncertainty. This would be the first time she'd ever revealed herself as a Muse to a mortal. Humanity had called on Muses throughout the ages, but she and her sisters had never done a damn thing to confirm their actual existence.

Risking a glance at Jax, she found his gaze locked on her face. He nodded, his brows raised in encouragement. "Clio, just spit it out."

She set the glass aside and twisted to face him. She slid one foot under the opposite leg and tucked the robe under her knee. Pressing a hand on his thigh, she took the plunge. "Jax, have you ever heard of the Muses?"

"You mean like the band?"

She snorted. Terri was to blame for the techno-rocker's name. Clio remembered how her sister had laughed like a demented loon once that band had crashed onto the music scene.

Focus, dammit! She shook away the memory. "No, like the beings who serve to inspire people to achieve greatness in art, writing, or science."

Jax's smile dimples. "Ah, you're talking about mythology."

Grasping his hand, she pulled it to her face and cupped it around her cheek. "Do I feel like a myth to you?"

"Huh?"

"Jax, I'm Clio, the Muse of History. Oh, and guitar."
She tipped her chin up. "I've been nudging generals,
statesmen, and inventors for thousands of years, inspiring
them to achieve their destinies. And then I record their
triumphs and defeats."

He drew his brows together and leaned away. She'd
pretend his withdrawal didn't sting like a painful spider
bite. Mouth opening and closing, it looked as though he
was trying to understand a completely foreign language.

A smile broke out on his face, but it never reached his
eyes. His laugh came out a skeptical, scoffing grunt. "Good
one, Clio. You had me going there."

"I'm serious, Jax. I'm a Muse. From ancient Greek
mythology…except we're real. We exist. My eight sisters
are all Muses as well."

"You don't look a day over twenty-five. So, I'm going
to say false." Pulling his palm from her cheek, he leaned
forward and grabbed the tumbler. His hand trembled
slightly when he lifted it. He took a hasty gulp of whiskey,
then coughed as he replaced the glass on the table.

"Add about eight thousand years, and you're in the
neighborhood of my exact age." Of course he wouldn't
believe her. She sounded bat-shit crazy, even to herself.
"I'm not insane. And I'm not making this up. Go ahead—
ask me about any event in history. From any time period.
I've either inspired it, witnessed it, or recorded it."

Jax popped off the sofa. Running his hand through his
hair, he paced in front of the unlit fireplace. "Fine. What
exactly happened with the Black Hole of Calcutta?"

Easy-peasy. She knew this incident well. "When Fort
William fell to the Nawab of Bengal, the British and
Anglo-Indian troops who'd remained to defend it were
imprisoned in a single cell, measuring four by five meters.
According to some accounts, as many as one-hundred-
forty-three men were jammed into a cell smaller than this

room. But the actual number was closer to seventy."
Conditions in the cell had been crushing, suffocating.
Pressure built in Clio's chest just thinking about it. "The
Nawab claimed he had no knowledge of the situation, but
in truth, he'd ordered the incarceration. Only twenty-three
survived the night."

"Lucky guess." He rubbed his eyes and puffed out his
cheeks. The motion caused his sexy dimples to play peek-a-
boo with her heart. Pausing from his pacing, he squinted at
her. "Okay, what about Genghis Khan's conquest of
Eastern Europe?"

"Genghis didn't lead the Mongol army into Europe.
His generals invaded Russia, Crimea, Armenia, and
Georgia while the Khan returned to Mongolia. What isn't
clear in the history books is that Khan was as much a
statesman as Thomas Jefferson, Ronald Reagan, or Mikhail
Gorbachev." It wasn't recorded properly because she'd
been distracted by King John signing the Magna Carta.
"Khan united the Silk Road under one cohesive political
system."

Jax gaze sharpened, his knuckles white when he
propped his fist on a hip.

She gripped the neck of her robe closed and watched
as he resumed his frantic pacing. "Are you convinced yet?"

"Those are facts anyone could know." The lack of
certainty in his voice led Clio to believe Jax might be
buying in to her story.

"That's true." Clio went for the score. Something no
one could know but would convince a history professor that
she'd been there. "In 1918, hours before the assassination
of the imperial family of Tsar Nicholas the Second, the
Grand Duchess Anastasia was rescued from house arrest by
Sophia Tyutcheva. She'd been governess to the imperial
children. She'd been fired for speaking out against
Rasputin." Clio leaned forward. "Sophia hid Anastasia in
Paris until the end of the First World War. They later

moved to French Polynesia where they lived as mother and daughter until Sophia's death in the late Fifties."

"Clio, rumors about Anastasia are a dime a dozen." He shook his head and crossed one arm over his chest. His knuckles popped as he dug his fingers into his neck.

Clio rose. The only way to convince him would require her to betray a promise made so many years ago. She stood indecisively for a moment. In light of the circumstances, Clio was certain the gracious woman Anastasia had grown into would have forgiven her. She moved to her desk in the corner. The top drawer scraped a little as she pulled it open. With unerring accuracy, she depressed a slight protrusion along the left side. The back of the drawer popped open with a click. From deep within the hidden compartment, she drew out a crimson velvet pouch. It lay heavy in her hand as she returned to Jax's side.

She grasped Jax's hand and lifted it, facing up. "But this isn't a rumor." Upending the ancient monogrammed bag over his outstretched palm, the weighty contents dropped with a quiet *thud*. The ornate brooch had a massive sapphire center. Sparkling crystals and diamonds surrounded the central stone. Another teardrop sapphire, the size of a robin's egg, swung freely at the bottom of the ornamental pin.

She pointed to the glittering piece. "This was Tsarina Alexandra's brooch. She wore it in all of her official portraits, including the one completed just days before her murder. It was one of the jewels never recovered from Alexandra's personal effects. Because she'd given this piece and several others to Sophia to help finance the escape of her children."

"I've seen pictures of this piece." Jax stared at the magnificent jewel in his hand. When he lifted his gaze to her, his eyes were clouded with doubt. "But all the children died."

Clio shook her head gently and folded Jax's fingers

over the top of the brooch. "Not all. I was with Anastasia when she actually died in 1974. She is buried next to Sophia on Marquesas Island in a cemetery overlooking the sea." She switched to the ancient language she'd heard him using as he sang in the library. "The name on her tombstone is Alix Hesse, her own mother's birth name."

She took a step away to give him space to process the words she'd spoken in a forgotten tongue and the proof she'd offered. She laid the velvet pouch on the table. Leaving her gaze on Jax, waiting for a response, she sat down.

Jax twirled the teardrop sapphire between his thumb and forefinger, his brows drawn up as he studied the piece. If his expression was a clue, it appeared he'd come to a conclusion about the truth of her story. He'd believe her, or he wouldn't. If she were meant to become a magpie, she'd know in the next few minutes.

Chapter 9

The brooch was solid in his hand. Either she was crazy, or he was. The cut, color, and setting had been accurately portrayed in official portraits. He'd never believed he'd be lucky enough to hold a piece of history like this in his hands. Jax remained standing, still as a statue. The unbelievable truth of what Clio had told him sat heavily on his shoulders. He scrabbled about in his brain for an alternate explanation.

Finally, he scrubbed his hand over his face. His thoughts spun as if he'd fallen into the rabbit hole.

He muttered, "I know this jewel. I know the names." He turned the brooch in his hand and peered at the jeweler's mark below the clasp. The line of Cyrillic symbols that represented Faberge's official mark had been stamped into the back of the brooch. The AH mark, representing the chief imperial jeweler August Holmstrom, had been imprinted just below the Faberge string. The piece weighed heavier in his hand due to its authenticity.

He lifted his gaze. He sucked in a deep breath and exhaled sharply. "And a gaping hole in a remarkable story has just been plugged." He reared back and searched the room for hidden cameras or men with white jackets and maybe a Taser meant to calm the lunatic. God, was he really going to say it? "Okay, I'm a believer."

Relief crashed over her face. "Thank you."

He laid the jewel on top of the scrap of velvet. Unable

to resist, he ran a fingertip over the imperial seal embroidered on the bag. Wonder and giddy excitement filled his heart as he took his seat next to her on the sofa. There were so many gaps in history she could fill.

A thousand questions rattled around his brain. "So, was Beowulf real?"

"Nope. He was only a legend with no basis in reality. Someone got a little tipsy on the mead and spun a great tale."

"Did Nero really fiddle while Rome burned?"

She nodded. "Uh-huh."

"Do you know how the pyramids were really built?"

She narrowed her eyes. "Jax, I'm happy to answer any of your questions, but we have a big problem."

And damn, that sexy squint fired his blood and made his dick jump to attention. Battling to get his body under control, he grasped her hand and asked his next question. "And…and what about Stonehenge? Were you there for the first equinox?"

"I just— Didn't you feel—?" A fast frown crinkled her features. "That is so weird. I just *suggested* to you that you stop asking questions so we could focus on the task at hand. But you kept asking questions. Didn't you feel the urging?"

"You can do that? Influence me that way?"

"Jax, I'm a Muse. My specialty is influencing people. How could you not respond to it?" She curled her lips in, capturing them between her teeth.

She could control his actions? His brain reeled in pace with his libido. "I felt an urge, but the task I had in mind seems vastly different than what you suggested."

"What did you feel?"

His cock hardened again. "Um, aroused. Ready to drag you back to the bedroom." Knowing hers would follow, he dropped his gaze to the bulge in his lap. When he looked up, her lips were parted and pink had flooded her cheeks.

She rubbed her temples "This has never happened before."

"How was I supposed to react?"

"It depends on what problem we're addressing. Most people embrace the prompt I send. Over the years, everyone else has reacted positively. For example, I nudged William Wallace to use the terrain to his advantage in the Battle of Stirling Bridge. He followed my idea, and the Scots soundly defeated King Edward's army."

"So, I'm just supposed to ignore my instincts and listen to the urgings I hear in my head? Your urgings?"

"Exactly." She captured her bottom lip between her teeth. His mouth went dry as the need to suck that same lip claimed him. She released her bite and held his gaze. "Let me try another suggestion. This time while I touch you."

Her palm was warm when she laced their fingers together. Narrowing her eyes, she stared straight at him.

A tingling started in his balls, then a surge of pressure speared his dick, turning it to steel. He nearly shot his wad off in his pants. "Oh, Jesus!" He jerked his hand from hers. Breaking the point of contact should have eased the insane need to push her to the cushions and pound into her in a fast, hard coupling. *Should have.*

"Jax?"

He leaped off the couch and moved gingerly to the fireplace, his back to her. "I need a minute." His entire body shuddered as he fought the desire swamping him. His knuckles turned white as he gripped the limestone mantel.

Behind him, he heard her stand. Something clattered on the table. Her steps were quiet on the rug, but slapped against the stone hearth when she joined him in front of the fireplace. She set his tumbler down, refraining from touching him, as if she understood the urges he battled. He swiped up the glass and drained it in one long swallow. Fire of a different kind filled his blood. She set her own drink down in front of him, then moved away three steps.

He gulped the contents of the second glass. "God, Clio. What the hell? It was ten times stronger when you touched me. Do your nudges affect every man like this?" Jealousy chewed the base of his neck. He hated the idea that other men might have similar reactions. He didn't want to think of any other man touching her.

"Jax, I've been pushing mortals for centuries, and I promise you, this has never happened before."

He heaved a relieved sigh. "Thank God."

Finally getting control of his body, he twisted around to face her.

Her brows were threaded together, her red-gold hair framing her face in a curly jumble. "Um, maybe it's better if I don't try to mentally suggest anything to you."

He barked out a laugh. "Good idea. At least for the time being. But feel free to nudge away after we talk about whatever you think we need to discuss." Because, Jesus God. Burying himself in her after one of her suggestions was guaranteed to blow his mind.

She moved away from him and sat in the wing chair opposite the couch. She gestured to the sofa, inviting him to take a seat. "I know you're familiar with The Five Nations Block."

Instant soft-on. The last thing he wanted to talk about was the conglomerate of countries intent on claiming someone else's corner of the world as theirs. He deflected her statement with a question. "Clio, what do they have to do with the problem you think we have?"

Her gaze never left his face. "Everything. The Block is up to something. They've been moving troops and repositioning artillery along their borders." He wished she'd tell him something he didn't know. She rubbed her arms. "It's up to us to stop them from encroaching on a smaller country."

"I've already tried. The Five Nations was my specialty at the think tank. The powers-that-be in our government want a peaceful solution to their aggression." God knew, he'd worked for years to get the bureaucratic idiots to hear his ideas. He could have circumvented the problem long ago if he'd been able to make the right people listen. The government's idea of a diplomatic solution only served to edge the world closer to a massive war. "I couldn't convince anyone to consider the logical alternative, a negotiated settlement where the Bulgarian people are protected. There is no stopping the Five Nations." The statement alone made his gut churn.

"There has to be." Clio rose from her seat, moved to her desk, and retrieved a scrap of paper. With graceful movements, she returned to his side. She handed him the document. "You need to read this. It will change your mind."

Battling the skepticism that had been his hallmark since he'd left GeoPoly, he took the sheet from her hand. It was an e-mail. The chilling message mentioned destruction, war, and an end to mankind. "Who is this Pierus?"

"He's a demi-god who thought his nine daughters were better than the daughters of Zeus, my sisters and me." The corners of her mouth lifted slightly. "Zeus is never nice when he's pissed off. He turned Pierus's daughters into magpies. Pierus has been seeking to restore them ever since."

"Whoa! Zeus is your dad? Like, Zeus Zeus? God of Gods, Zeus?" Okay, his world shifted from *I can handle her as a Muse* to *what the fuck have I gotten myself into*? He shook his head in denial but then recalled the sight of the bird this morning, and more recently outside Clio's bedroom window.

"The same. Anyway, Pierus resurfaced recently and challenged us to a contest to return his brats to human form. It's his version of a hostile takeover of Olympus. He wins, and he gets dominion over all immortals. And his daughters would be unleashed on humanity." Clio shuddered. "The effect on mortals will be dire. They'll live up to their names, like Tyranny, Strife, Mayhem. You get the idea."

"Can he do it?" Aw, shit. That sounded like he was a believer. And maybe, just maybe...

Clio frowned. "He can if we fail at the challenge he's set for us."

"Have any of you failed?"

She shrugged. "I'm the first."

"His message says one Muse, one man. How do you know I'm the man?"

"The magpies keep appearing. You mentioned a run in with a crazy old man and a bird. I believe that was Pierus. The other night in the library when it was storming so badly, I spied the image of Pierus and his skanky daughter in a flash of lightning." She shook her head again. "Tonight when we walked past the street musician, that was Pierus in disguise."

The dotted line from his run-in with the bird to Clio's story just filled in like a solid fucking black dart.

"I put money in that guy's case. Does that mean something?" What if he'd set something into motion by unwittingly supporting this Pierus dude's cause? His gut cramped.

Her smile was gentle. "It only means you are a decent, generous human being."

Being a good human didn't help win epic battles. Being compassionate didn't equal persuasive. "Clio, I can't make anyone listen to me. I don't have that kind of influence in Washington."

"Jax, I think the daughter I must defeat is Tyranny. If The Five Nations invade the smaller country they surround and unify into one solid block, like the old Soviet Union, there will be no stopping their conquering ways."

"But if my suggestions are interpreted the wrong way, it won't matter." The horror of the blood diamond fiasco washed over him like an unrelenting riptide.

Her gaze was steadfast. "We won't know if we don't try. Jax, if I lose, life for all mortals will irrevocably change for the worse. As gods, we've loved and protected humankind for thousands of years. Our ability to save them will disappear." There was no plea in her voice. Just matter-of-fact sincerity.

"Clio, when I met Peter Russell—that's the name the crazy old bastard gave me—he knew about my involvement in a situation with blood diamonds. I'd advised our government to remain neutral in the domestic struggle in Sierra Leone, to try a humanitarian strategy." He toyed with the bottom of his shirttail, rolling it up and unrolling it again. "My recommendation resulted in an unforgivable loss of life. People were slaughtered in the conflict."

"That won't happen this time." Her tone held a note of uncertainty.

"But what if it does?" It seemed the only answer to his *what if* was doubt.

"If it does, then my existence will cease. It will only take me, or one of my sisters, to lose the contest for Pierus to take over. My loss would result in an entire country and its citizens becoming slaves. Who knows what will happen with the other Muses' challenges? Eventually, Pierus's domination will expand to all mortals. People shouldn't have to suffer because we didn't try."

His heart felt as though it was caught in a vise, the pressure crushing. He didn't want her to vanish from his life. But he didn't know if he could conquer his doubts long enough to make a difference. *Yet you believe this woman across from you is a mythological being.*

The bruising grip on his heart reminded him. "When I was talking to Peter, or Pierus, I think he nudged me the way you do. Except instead of pleasure, the result was agonizing. Like he was squeezing my brain between his hands."

"His influence would be different than mine, but it shouldn't hurt." She steepled her fingers and pressed them to her lips. "When a nudge runs up against resistance, I guess it could be painful. But I've never heard of it happening. Of course, I've never seen a prod affect a man bodily the way mine did with you."

Jax stood and started buttoning his shirt. The rabbit hole he'd fallen into spun like a top. He'd met a demi-god intent on conquering and enslaving the world. He'd slept with a woman who was a Muse. And the sex had been inspiring. But the top of his head was going to blow off if he didn't put some distance between this challenge and his normal life.

"I can't give you an answer now, Clio. This is so much to take in. I need time to process it. To come up with a strategy."

She scrunched her eyes again. "We don't have much time, Jax."

Something shifted in his chest instead of his pants. But that sweet tingling sensation was present again. "You just tried to poke me again." The accusation hung in the air between them.

A becoming shade of pink flooded her cheeks. "I need you to help me, Jax. Without me and my sisters, the world will become a bleak, awful place. No creativity, no art or music or dance. Who would record history and render it accurately in my stead?" She shook her head. "Plus, I do not want to be a magpie for eternity. That's a long, long time."

He moved toward her until he stood directly in front of the chair she hadn't left. Bracing his hands on the arms of the wingback, he bent to kiss her. His lips cut off any further comment she might have made. He stroked his tongue around her lips and then slipped it inside her mouth. The palm of her hand was warm and comfortable when she cupped his jaw. She returned the kiss with a fervor that matched his.

He broke the seal between them, then dipped back in and pressed his mouth to the corner of hers. He rested his forehead against hers. "I didn't say I wouldn't help. But I need time to figure this out. Can you give me a couple of days?"

She released a sigh, her breath caressing his cheek. "I'd give you a lifetime if we had it. Please don't think too long, Jax. The world needs you." She stroked her fingertips over his cheek and held his gaze. "I need you."

Chapter 10

I n his lonely bedroom, Jax awoke and kicked himself for leaving Clio's house. He'd declined her invitation to stay over, fabricating an early meeting as an excuse. A shadow had flickered in her eyes when he'd said he had to leave. It had almost made him change his mind. He didn't have any such engagement, but he'd needed time to process everything she'd revealed to him. When he'd wavered, she'd smiled sadly and pushed him out the door.

Her claim to be a Muse would be intriguing to anyone. A thousands-of-years-old being who'd influenced the world in the most unique way. As a historian, the idea was as mind blowing as the sex had been. His job was to interpret the writings of people who'd made history, to enlighten his students about what had happened. If Clio was to be believed, she'd been present as history was being made. And she'd recorded history for years, generations to come.

He might be fucked in the head, but he believed her. The brooch had been the one detail that had tipped the scale in her favor. There was no denying the veracity of the Faberge mark on the back of the piece.

Last night he'd powered up his laptop within minutes of walking through his front door. The image search he'd done had confirmed what he already knew. The brooch appeared in almost every official portrait of Alexandra. It was recorded as missing on the archival list of the Imperial Family's personal effects. He was blown away by the fact he'd held the lost piece of history in his hand for a short time last night.

The clock on his bedside table ticked steadily as he lay on his back. With his head on the pillow, one arm slung across his forehead, he'd hugged another pillow and wished Clio's warm, pliant body occupied the space next to him. God, she might be mad as a hatter, but he dug her brand of crazy.

Dust motes swam in the rays of light shining through his blinds. At least it was sunny outside. The light hit the pile of clothes he'd left in the corner. He needed a trip to a Laundromat, or to the appliance store to buy a washer and dryer. On top of the pile was an old sky-blue T-shirt he'd worn to the university's rec center. The shade almost matched the color Clio's eyes had glowed in the candlelight at the restaurant last night.

His phone chirped with an incoming text.

With a grunt, he rolled to his side. Shoving an arm under the pillow, he propped his head up. Anticipation climbed along his spine. It could be Clio. He snatched the phone from the bedside table, depressed the menu button, and tapped in his passcode. A message from his former boss popped up, begging him to contact her at the think tank as quickly as possible.

He debated returning the call right away but decided hitting the shower was more important than hitting the return call command. The phone bounced when he tossed it on the mattress. Scratching his chest, he padded into the bathroom. As he closed the door, the phone pinged again. He might regret it, but he was going to douse himself in cold, head-clearing water before tackling a conversation with his old employer.

Fifteen minutes later, he shoved his legs into a pair of jeans. Finger combing his hair, he moved toward the bed. He swept up his phone, jerked the comforter back into place, and then left his bedroom.

In the kitchen, he grabbed a glass from the cabinet. The cranapple juice sparkled in the light from the window over the sink. While his sugary, carb-loaded breakfast, cinnamon sugar Pop-Tarts, toasted, he finally looked at his phone.

Three more texts had come in while he'd showered. Disappointed that none were from Clio, he opened the last one. As he started to read the urgent message, the phone rang. The main number for the think tank displayed on the screen.

"You're in a God-awful rush to get in touch with me today, aren't you?" he asked in lieu of a greeting. "What's set your world on fire, Beryl?"

"Have you stopped watching the news since you left DC, love?" Beryl's voice purred in his ear.

She'd always had a sexy, deep rasp when she spoke to him. When she'd whispered her first invitation to her bed, that voice had stroked his imagination and his libido. Now, it left him cold. Beryl might have been a friend with benefits, but by the end of his tenure with GeoPoly, she'd been no friend.

He pushed away the memory of her long legs, athlete's body, and her deliberate lack of support in the final month of his employment. "Of course not," he answered. "I've been busy getting settled here. Haven't tuned in for the past twenty-four hours. What have I missed?" Other than a chance to wake with Clio in his arms this morning. He sipped his juice and waited for her reply.

"The Five Nations is on the move. As you predicted." Her voice now held more of a peeved tone than its normal sex-kitten purr.

His shoulders tensed. His predictions had been dire. "Have they hit the mountain road?"

"That was their first move. From what we can detect on aerial photos, a refugee camp at the Bulgarian border has been razed." Her dry, matter-of-fact comment pissed him off. Her delivery was distinctly inhumane considering she'd just relayed the fact that thousands of asylum seekers had been murdered.

The fact his warning had come true made his gut pitch and roll like a helicopter without a gyroscope. He'd pleaded with Beryl and her immediate boss to step in with a sure-fire diplomatic solution. His idea would have saved all those innocent lives.

He clenched his fist and slammed it toward the counter, slowing his trajectory at the last second so he barely tapped the Formica top. Pinching pain grabbed him behind the eyes, making his entire head ache.

"Bet you're sorry you didn't listen to me sooner." He couldn't help baiting her. Any hope for a peaceful resolution seemed unattainable at this stage in the game.

"Let's not get into a pissing contest here, Jax. We're ready to listen now. We need your help."

He scoffed. "What if I don't want to help?"

"I know you better than that." The purr was back in her voice.

Helping Beryl would help Clio as well. And that fact was more persuasive than anything Beryl, or her boss, or even the President himself, could offer. He'd do it to save Clio from an eternity as a disgusting, squawking bird.

He bent at the waist, propped an elbow on the counter, and rested his forehead in his hand. Was he crazy to believe in the Muses? In gods and goddesses? He pushed the thought to the back of his mind as the seconds of weighty silence spun between them.

"Jax?" Was that fright he heard in Beryl's pinched voice?

"If I help, it has to be on my terms," he told her. "You'll come to me. And you'll implement whatever solutions I deliver. And I have free range to bring in whomever I need to accomplish the task. Understood?"

"I'm not sure I can agree to those terms."

"Then we don't have a deal. Goodbye, Beryl. And good luck." Jax rarely played politics and less frequently played hardball, but when he did, he pulled out his balls of steel and a cast-iron cup for his jock strap.

"Wait!" Panic edged her voice. "Fine, I'll convince everyone we have to do it this way. Tell me when and where to show up, and I'll bring the whole damn tank to you."

God, he liked winning.

If she brought the whole department, they'd need a decent size space to work in. One that could offer privacy and the level of available technology that would support their operation. The Ancient Civ room at the DCU library was exactly the spot they needed.

"We do this in Delphi." Where he could keep Clio safe from a future as a bird. He hoped. "I'll need you to contact a couple of people and grease the cogs. And you'd better tell your tech staff they'll need to go wheels up by the end of the day."

"Just fax me a list of people I need to contact. The plan is already in motion. Your secure log-in to the system has been restored. You'll need a couple of hours to get through the latest reports."

"You were pretty damn confident I'd do this, weren't you?"

"I'd hoped," she said. After the space of several heartbeats, she continued, "I've missed you, lover."

"Let's get one thing straight, Beryl. I'm not your lover anymore. We're more over than that sad reality TV program you liked to watch."

"We'll see, Jax. We shall see."

As far as he was concerned, there was nothing left to see. He shoved the juice back into the fridge. Sex with Beryl had been cold, almost robotic. Touch here, stroke there, moan loudly, dig deeper, insert tab A into slot B. The woman had known how to manipulate his tab. But that was no way to have a love affair as far as he was concerned. Like he was nothing but a—a tool.

With Clio, every second, every movement, every breathy sigh and satisfied moan, had been spontaneous and energizing. That was what he was looking for in his life. He found he craved the woman as much as he craved the sex.

He started a pot of coffee. While the rich, aromatic blend brewed, he powered up his laptop. Even though it was July, the morning was cool enough to sit on his screened front porch and catch up on the entire Bulgarian situation. Without the complete background, he'd never find a solution that worked for all parties involved. And finding a workable resolution when the governments of six nations were in play might be harder than finding Waldo, or solving one of those Magic Eye puzzles.

By noon he was wiping sweat from his brow. The climbing temp forced him to relocate inside his air-conditioned house. Sitting at his kitchen table, he'd made a reasonable dent in the mountain of documentation on the secure server. Most of the information was useless, just snippets of conversations or e-mails that some security agency had flagged as suspect. But a few trends began to coalesce. Recognizable patterns fell into place like a jigsaw puzzle.

But frustration mounted as he continued to miss something from the big picture. The work was numbingly tedious and his back, shoulders, and ass ached from sitting still for so long.

Someone pounded on his front door, and he heard it open before he could rise to answer the summons. Only one person he knew would be bold enough to enter his home without an invitation.

"Jax? Dude, are you here?" Ian's voice echoed from the front door all the way to his kitchen.

"Back here," he shouted. He arched back in his chair and rubbed his stinging eyes. He'd been staring at the screen entirely too long.

Ian sauntered into the room. "Buddy, you should answer your phone occasionally. I've called once an hour since nine this morning."

Jax cast a glance around the kitchen. The pastry box and toaster still littered the counter. But no phone. Where had he left it? "Didn't hear it ring, man. And when did you turn into a fucking needy girl. Calling every hour?"

"Someone has to watch out for you."

"And you nominated yourself?" Jax smirked. Ian had been looking out for him since college. "I got kind of buried under a project. What'd you need?"

Ian propped his back against the refrigerator and cocked his head. "Just checking in on you. Thought I'd see if you wanted to grab a bite to eat and catch the Demons game. First pitch is at three-thirty."

"Ah, God. I can't." He scrubbed a hand over his face then curled it around his neck, massaging the tight, knotted muscles. His stomach rumbled at the thought of food. Had he eaten anything since his Pop-Tarts breakfast?

Ian pointed at Jax's belly. "I heard that. What the hell are you working on, anyway?"

Jax looked at his laptop where he had at least twenty different windows open. The dock at the bottom stretched across his entire screen, the icons miniscule. He pulled out the pen he'd stuck behind his ear and began flipping it around and over the back of his knuckles. "Nothing."

Ian barked out a short laugh. "Gotta call bullshit on that. Your eyes are bloodshot, like you've been staring at the screen too long. Is it porn?"

Resting a hand on his belly, Jax heaved a big fucking sigh. "I wish. Dammit, I got sucked back in."

"To GeoPoly?"

Jax nodded as he shoved his chair back. He stood next to the table and tried to rub sensation back into his ass.

"Aw, shit. You worked so hard to leave that behind. Is

this about the Five Nations' sudden aggression?"

"Watched the news, did you?" Jax hadn't turned it on all day. Typically, the media distorted facts, and honestly, he didn't need the distraction.

"Haven't you?" Ian stared intently at him, brows arched high, as if he'd never seen Jax before. Or this incarnation of him.

"What the big five bastards have been doing in the past few days is anything but sudden. This clusterfuck has been on a slow simmer for years. It is a little odd that they've taken action at all. What made them move now?" That was the piece of information that Jax couldn't find. A thought niggled at the base of his skull. Maybe the accelerated aggression had a supernatural cause. Could Pierus be behind it? He cast his glance to the counter again, seeking his phone. He needed to talk to Clio about the possibility.

"The reports aren't clear about that. But every media outlet has dedicated their entire broadcast to the situation. By the fourth time you see a clip of the carnage, it's almost old news. By the twenty-seventh, you just want to throw shit at the TV."

"Truth." Jax twisted his torso from side-to-side. His back creaked as he released the residual stiffness.

"Got any beer?" Ian pushed away from the fridge. He jerked the door open and bent to reach for a bottle. He started laughing. "Jesus, Jax. You really were sucked in." He righted himself and waggled Jax's cell phone between his fingers.

"I don't remember putting that in there. But it explains why I never heard your calls."

Ian tossed the phone to Jax. "Mine, or six others."

Shit, he had missed a lot of calls. But at least the people who'd called from the think tank had e-mailed their questions and comments when he'd failed to answer.

He quickly scrolled through the alerts on his home screen. Clio still hadn't reached out to him. Disappointment and hurt flared in his gut. Christ! Who was being a fucking needy girl now? He pushed the sensation away as he accepted an opened Heineken from Ian.

He took a long, satisfying pull from the bottle.

Ian tipped his beer Jax's direction. "So, lunch?"

"What the hell. I deserve a break. Finish your beer while I answer this one e-mail from Beryl. She's looking for a place to stay when she blows into town tomorrow."

"Wait a second! Beryl the Ball-buster is coming here?" Ian muttered a coarse word under his breath. The first time they'd met, Ian had developed a case of insta-hate for Beryl.

"Yeah. They wanted me in DC, but I can't leave right now."

"Would this have anything to do with a red-headed goddess named Clio?"

"How the fuck do you know that?" Had Clio already confided in Ian? Or maybe the reporter sister Ian had mentioned had shared the information with him. How many people knew Muses actually existed?

"Dude, you should see your face when you talk about her. It's like you're blinded by her light or something. If she's half as hot as her sister, Polly, then she'd have to be a goddess."

Jax eased out a breath. It appeared Clio's secret was still safe. "Well, she is pretty hot." And insanely smart, and everything else that got Jax's motor revving. That, and the fact her nudges affected his other head in the most delightful way.

But what if the attraction he felt for her was only because of her mental prodding? Had she influenced him to fall for her? What if a relationship between them was part of a bigger scam to get him to help? She wouldn't do that, would she?

He brushed the doubt from his mind and focused on the e-mail he needed to send. "So, can you recommend a hotel in Delphi?? Because Beryl is most definitely not welcome to stay here."

"Send her to the Athenian. It's nice, and the head groundskeeper is a hound. Maybe he'll take some of her edge off."

Jax snorted out a laugh. No way in hell would anything, or anyone, reduce Beryl's sexual appetite. But he'd leave it to someone else to try. Because for the foreseeable future, the only edge he had any interest in was Clio's.

Chapter 11

"You don't look so good," Nia crooned as she slid onto the cane-backed chair across the café table from Clio. "Are you okay?"

Ah, the sixty-four-billion-dollar question. "For crying out loud, Nia. Why don't you just tell me I look like shit?" She rubbed her bleary eyes. Her middle child angst reared its ugly head, making her regret her harsh words. "Sorry, I didn't sleep well last night. I… This challenge has me out of sorts."

After she'd told Jax about being a Muse, he'd claimed an early morning meeting as a reason to not stay over. A tidy lie she'd chosen to believe, but nonetheless it had made her feel a little cheap and a lot dirty. And he'd resisted the idea of helping her with the challenge. Clio had fretted most of the night away. She worried she'd revealed too much. Or not enough.

It wasn't like the damn task ahead came with a road map.

She took a sip from her coffee cup. The scalding liquid burned her lip, and she couldn't help wishing Jax were around to kiss the sting away.

"Hey, I wasn't trying to be mean. I'm not Callie." Nia curled her lips, part smirk, part grin. "So why didn't you sleep?"

"I had a date with Jax last night—"

"What? Did you do the dirty?" Nia's screechy voice

drew attention from the other patrons at the coffee shop.

Mortified heat swept up Clio's face. She hit her sister with a silencing jab.

"Ouch." Nia pressed shaky fingers to her temple in response.

"Be quiet. We are not going to talk about my sex life in The Daily Grind." One nice perk of being a Muse was the ability to influence large groups of people. Clio broadcasted a mental message to everyone present to ignore what Nia had said and just go about their business. Once again, conversation rose from the tables surrounding them.

Nia's coppery curls glinted as she bobbed her head. "Sorry. I was excited for you. But if you didn't sleep, it explains your haggard appearance."

"I had to tell Jax who I am, and why he needs to help. Except my nudges didn't work on him. I've never had that happen before. I had no choice but to explain I'm a Muse."

Nia's mouth popped open and her eyes widened, making her look like a Bratz doll. "Oh, my goddess. How did he take it?"

"A lot better than I'd imagined. Seriously, most people would have called the asylum to arrange an immediate one-way ride to straight-jacket-ville. But Jax just took it all in stride."

"Will he help?"

The shop door opened, admitting a blast of hot air and Polly. She waved to them and pointed to the barista as she proceeded to the counter.

"Don't know. I'll explain after Polly gets her coffee." Clio broke off a corner of her cranberry-orange scone and popped it into her mouth. Mmm, other than the salt on Jax's skin, this was her favorite flavor in the world.

Joining them, Polly set her cup and saucer down. She dropped her oversize purse to the ground with a loud *thunk* and scraped the legs of her chair across the shiny cement floor.

"Girl, you can't do anything quietly, can you?" Clio bit out. She immediately regretted her tone and attempted to soothe it with a tight smile.

Polly shrugged and dropped into her seat. "Want the world to know I'm around." She took a sip of her tea—her eyes alight with merriment over the rim of the cup. She'd always been the loudest one in the family. And in a household of nine girls, that was saying something. The trait had served her well in crowded press conferences. She always got a chance to ask her question.

"Okay, now she's here, Clio. You can finish telling about your night with the hunky Professor Callahan." Nia waggled her brows as she spoke.

Polly set her cup down with a rattle. "You and the hot prof did it?"

"Holy Hades, you two. You are awful." Best to just put it out there so they could move on. "Yes, I did sleep with Jax. And yes, it was better than awesome. Maybe even the best in centuries. Now, can we get back to the goddessdamn challenge?"

"Good for you, Clio. You deserve to be sexed up properly. Goddess knows, it's been too long." Polly patted Clio's hand. A genuinely happy smile lit her sister's face, reaching her eyes. Polly finally put her phone face down on the table. "There's a report of torrential rains in what is normally the dry season in Bulgaria. The Five Nations army occupies high ground. The storm gave them an advantage. Nia, have you discovered anything about the weather patterns?"

Nia spoke up. "I've researched the crazy storms we've been having. Cross-referenced it with world events. I can't find any instances of similar patterns in the National Oceanic and Atmospheric Administration's documentation. In addition to NOAA's data, I looked at the United Nations' archives and came up with a big fat goose egg there as well." A smile slid across her wide mouth. "I should have started with the archives in Olympus. Because I found a gold-mine there."

Clio leaned forward, impatient to know what her sister knew. "Don't keep us in suspense, Nia."

"In the fifteen hundreds, when Spain ejected Jews and Muslims, there were anecdotal reports of tornadoes, floods, and landslides. There might have even been an earthquake or two. I found two separate footnotes linking the unnatural events to Guabancex."

Clio pushed her cold coffee away. The dread in her soul frosted her blood. "Why the freak would the Taino storm gods be involved?"

Nia shrugged. "I bet if we dug deep enough, we'd find some connection between them and Pierus. There is definitely some sort of conspiracy here."

Clio pressed her clenched fist to her mouth. Tension in the region of The Five Nations had gone on forever. It never occurred to her that Pierus was doing anything to escalate it.

Polly stuffed her phone back in her bag. "Drill down to the roots if necessary. We need to find the link if we want to circumvent the death of so many innocents and keep Clio from becoming a pesky magpie." She slurped the last of her tea then set the cup on the saucer with a distinctive *clack*. "I have to get to the newsroom. I'll see you tonight at the Athenian. Togas optional."

"I have to go, too." Nia hitched the strap of her purse over her shoulder. She stood when Polly rose. "Don't worry too much, Clio. We'll work this out."

Nia and Polly each kissed one of Clio's cheeks. As they exited the shop, Clio propped her elbow on the table and rested her chin in her hand. The meeting with her parents tonight was bound to be brutal. Gaia never missed much. As Clio was Zeus's favorite, her relationship with Jax, a mortal man, would be subject to her father's laser-like attention.

But she'd have to bear it because there'd be Hades to pay if she missed the meeting and blew her task of saving the world. Life had been much simpler when she was only a librarian.

Chapter 12

C lio steered her Mini Cooper into a space in the lot next to the Athenian. She wasn't late, but all her sisters had already arrived, judging by the cars present. She scrambled out of the car and trotted across the tarmac. She could have shifted through the Hollow and arrived faster, but it was a pleasant evening for a drive. And since it could be one of the last pleasant nights she'd have, she was damn sure going to take advantage of it.

Her parent's resort was on the south side of town, on the edge of an enchanting woodland, bordered on one side by a wide river. She and her sisters had grown up on the property and learned to swim in the fast-flowing current. Of all her childhood homes, this ranked as one of her favorites. Until they came into their powers in each life cycle, they'd been allowed to roam free, riding horses as young girls and Vespas as teeny-boppers. Her mother had hosted many of their school dances in the ornate ballroom at the rear of the main building.

When they'd received their powers this time around, the ceremonies took place at a temple buried deep in the forest. The event hadn't been much more than an outdoor barbecue, after which Zeus and their godparents chanted a prayer over their heads. Each of them had celebrated their rite of passage at the space that doubled as a picnic area for resort guests.

Gripping her keys in one hand and her purse in the

other, Clio's footsteps lagged as she approached the resort's colonnaded front entry. Near the bottom of the steps lay a clump of black and white feathers. Noxious awareness slithered up her spine. Nerves jumbled around her belly. Tyranny was losing her feathers. Replacing them with what, though? They had to figure out a way to defeat Pierus. And she still hadn't spoken to Jax to see if he'd commit to helping.

The marble columns, topped with ionic scrolls common in many majestic old ruins, should have looked pretentious. But they fit with the rounded portico covering the front entrance. Polished stone gleamed in the late afternoon sun as she clambered up the steps.

"Daughter." Zeus' sonorous voice stopped her forward progress.

He'd traded his normal business suit for board shorts and a Hawaiian print shirt in orange, lime, and fuchsia. The informal dress was at odds with the severe style of his wavy, salt-and-pepper hair. At least he hadn't plucked laurel twigs from the nearby bush to weave a crown.

She jammed her hands on her hips and faced him where he sat on the gliding porch swing. She'd spent a lot of hours there with him. "I'm not late, Zeus. I'm five minutes early." Even though he referred to her as daughter, he'd never encouraged them to call him Father. And Dad had never fit with his role of CEO of the multinational conglomerate Olympus had evolved to. So Zeus it was.

"I know this, Clio." His low chuckle rumbled in his chest, and his deep violet eyes glittered with humor. "I came out here to wait for you for a proper hello before the rest of the hens start cackling." He tipped his chin up, revealing a tiny cut on the underside. Stubble she wasn't used to seeing encased his strong jaw.

She swept one index finger over the other, a non-verbal shame-on-you. "That's a lie. As soon as there was more than one of them in the library, that ship sailed." She sent him a sunny smile as she crossed the porch. The swing stirred gently when she took a seat next to him.

"As you'd say in this life cycle, 'busted.'" The sound of feminine laughter echoed through the open front door. Zeus grimaced. "Thalia is trying out a new comedy routine. I do believe this one is quite entertaining, but I don't understand some of the jokes."

"I only have four minutes now until I'm officially late and Calliope makes sure I know it. Zeus, you aren't waiting out here to escape Thalia's sense of humor. Why don't you tell me what's really on your mind?" She folded her hand into his.

"I am worried about this challenge you face. Pierus's insistence that you must have a man help you is perplexing. This has never been the case in all the millennia of our existence. Why the sudden shift?"

Clio shrugged. "Maybe he thinks the man destined to help us won't actually find us." Or maybe the dirty bastard believed if the Muse fell in love with the man, it would be easier to break their hearts and defeat them.

"I should have encased the little fucker in granite when I had the chance. Instead of magpies, I should have turned his daughters into guppies."

That made her laugh. But she sobered quickly. "I've found the man to help me. Jax Callahan."

He grasped her chin between his thumb and forefinger and urged her face his direction. "I know this as well, daughter. And have you lost your heart to him?"

Had she? She'd never felt the kind of magnetism she'd found in Jax's touch. Never experienced the type of passion he aroused in her. It was her job to inspire him, but she felt as though the sandal was on the other proverbial foot. Unlike her sisters, in all her lifetimes, she'd resisted love. Being reborn with every memory intact came with consequences, and she remembered every relationship and partner she'd ever had. Recalling previous loves was always be painful. Was it just the challenge that made Jax different?

Zeus inclined his head and waited patiently for her answer. She shook her head. "Don't know, but I might have."

"Clio, if you have found love, this is a good thing. It means you will work harder to win the challenge Pierus has thrown down. And this makes me happy, because of all my children, of you nine girls, to see you transformed into a bird for all eternity would break my heart." He pressed a gentle kiss to her forehead then drew her head to his shoulder.

The weight of his arm holding her close made her feel secure and protected, a comfort lacking since she first learned of the difficult task in front of her. The only other time she'd felt this had been in Jax's arms. She closed her eyes and breathed deep, willing the last shred of trepidation from her body. It wouldn't do to give in to uncertainty. Better to believe she'd win.

While they sat in silence, the sun sank behind gathering clouds. Another storm brewed for Delphi.

"There you are," Callie said from the door. For a change, she wore a gentle expression, instead of her normal my-way-or-the-highway scowl. "We're ready to get started if you are."

Zeus squeezed her shoulder. The old wooden swing gave a little as he disentangled himself and rose. Confidence oozed from his posture as he strode across the porch.

He paused next to Callie and patted her cheek. Zeus loved all his daughters, and he never failed to demonstrate his devotion with kisses and hugs. He hadn't always been around as they grew up, but they'd known of his affection for them. After Callie pressed her lips to his cheek, he disappeared inside.

Clio grasped her purse handles and rose from her seat.

Callie stopped Clio with a hand on her arm when she would have moved past. "I know I've been tough on all you girls lately, but I've been that way because I'm terrified for all of us."

It wasn't often that Clio found herself in a position to comfort her bossy older sibling. "We're all frightened, sister. But I believe we'll be okay. Together we are a power to be reckoned with. And with men we love at our side, we will defeat Pierus for all eternity." She hoped the emotion she felt for Jax was returned. But since he hadn't even committed to helping yet, she had to squelch that desire. If she had to find a way to win without Jax, she would.

She laced her fingers through Callie's and tugged her inside to join the rest of the Thanos women and one old, softie king of the Greek gods.

They moved into the resort's small conference room. Clio's sisters and their parents were seated around the oversize table that had served as the site of all their holiday meals. Instead of the china and crystal, pads of paper and pens littered the top. Thalia and Mel had their identical twin heads together in a whispered conversation. As Muses of Comedy and Tragedy, they looked alike, yet personality-wise, they were as different as salt and pepper.

Aerie doodled on a slip of paper. Of all her sisters, Aerie was the shyest. Which was funny because she was the Muse of Romantic Love. Her job as a wedding planner was perfect for her. Clio craned her head to see what Aerie had drawn, but beyond the outline of a heart, the scribbling wasn't obvious.

Nia looked up from her conversation with Polly as Clio slipped into the seat across from them. Both women gave her broad smiles and winks. Damn, she should have kept her mouth closed about her time with Jax. She sure as hell shouldn't have told them it was the best sex she'd had in a millennium.

She cast a quick glance toward Gaia, who bestowed a

calm, knowing smile that worked wonders to settle Clio's nerves. She held her mother's gaze and mouthed *I need to talk to you privately.*

Gaia nodded and mouthed back *After.*

Corie, Muse of Dance, and her musically inclined sister, Terri, sat at the far end of the table, to the right of the chair Zeus occupied. They bickered quietly about something. Clio couldn't hear the conversation over Thalia's sudden laughter. The musical sound lightened Clio's spirits.

Gaia rapped her knuckles on the table, bringing the meeting to order. Zeus might be at the head of the table, but this was Gaia's gig. He seemed content to let his lover take the lead. Clio settled her handbag on the floor and grabbed a pad from the stack in front of her. She stole the pen Polly had behind her ear.

Polly tried to snatch it back. "Bitch! Get your own."

Clio pulled her hand back, keeping the pen out of Polly's reach. "I promise to return it, stingy."

"Children," Gaia gently chided. "We have important things to discuss. Shall we get started? Clio, can you give us a report?"

Sucking in a deep breath, Clio began. "First you should know I believe the Tainos are involved as well. It appears Pierus might have forged an alliance with them. Kind of like despicable, silent partners."

"Dirty bastards," Callie muttered. "Of course he couldn't be in this alone."

Clio held up a hand. "Callie, we don't know for sure they're involved. Call it a hunch." But it was a pretty strong coincidence that couldn't be denied. "It's just...there have been so many freak storms in the past weeks. Here and in Bulgaria."

Silence reigned around the table as Zeus sat unnaturally still, head tipped back, his eyes closed. His shoulders lifted in a shrug an instant before his eyelids popped open. The residual golden glow faded from his eyes as he nodded. "Proceed, Clio."

"I found the man Pierus foretold. Or rather, he found me." Clio wondered briefly whom her father had been communicating with, but knew he'd tell them eventually. She leaned forward, propped her arms on the table, and tapped Polly's pen on the dark cherry surface. "However, I'm not sure he'll help."

"Why wouldn't he? Doesn't he want to save the world?" Mel demanded. Leave it to her to make it as dramatic, as potentially tragic, as she could.

Clio sent a quelling look toward Mel before continuing. "He's already advised the government on a diplomatic solution for The Five Nations build-up, but they didn't listen. And it isn't the first time they've disregarded his counsel. The last time resulted in a major loss of life. He's gun shy and no longer believes in his ability to make a difference."

Just saying the words caused anxiety to rattle her spine and settle like a boa constrictor around her throat. She hooked a finger in the collar of her navy-blue T-shirt and pulled it away from her neck, hoping to ease the choking, suffocating sensation.

Callie spoke up. "It does sound like he is the perfect candidate. We just need to figure out how to get him to believe in magic again."

Hanging her head, Clio made her confession. "I told him what I am."

"Daughter!" Gaia shot a worried glance at Zeus.

"I'm sorry. I know I probably shouldn't have, but I didn't feel I had a choice. He believes *I* believe I'm a Muse, but I'm still not sure he'll help."

Zeus shook his head. "We will worry about this breach of our ways later. If necessary, we'll enlist your auntie, Mnemosyne, to remove his recollection of your slip once the challenge is won."

If the goddess of memory got involved, would Jax forget her? Was that the danger she faced in winning the challenge? Would her heart ever heal in this lifetime or any future existences? If not, she'd almost rather be a magpie.

"And if he doesn't help?" Thalia asked, a tight frown furrowing her forehead. "Can we proceed without his assistance? Can we make a difference in the situation overseas?"

Ten pairs of eyes looked to their father for guidance. Zeus steepled his fingers and pressed them against his lips. His eyelids drifted shut as he contemplated the question.

Tension grew with the ongoing silence until Clio thought it might crush her lungs. "Pierus's e-mail only said we had to pair up with the man. To win the challenge, we must make him question *what if.* And reject a deep-seated belief. I might have already done that by getting him to believe I'm a Muse. If he believes that, he's already asking the magic question. He's a pragmatic history professor. Until last night, Muses were nothing more than a myth."

Zeus hummed, an ancient tune that all who knew him recognized as his consulting mantra. His lips moved as if he spoke to someone. The CEO of Olympus was using his supernatural link to talk to some other god about the situation.

Mel sipped her water and then carefully set the glass on the coaster in front of her. "It still doesn't solve the problem The Five Nations presents."

Clio clung to the idea that if Jax accepted her as a Muse, he'd accept his role in stopping the madness overseas and Pierus's hostile takeover bid. If she was asking him to believe in her, she had to believe in him.

Chapter 13

Zeus's eyes popped open. His smile broadened as he glanced around the table. "I do not know if Clio has already fulfilled the requirements. But I believe I have found a way to sway Professor Callahan's thoughts. At least on the subject of his ability to make a difference." He paused and shut his eyes again.

Clio chewed her lip while Zeus finished his silent sidebar conversation with whomever he'd contacted. She glanced at each of her sisters to find their attention glued to their father. Gaia, on the other hand, stared straight at Clio. Her mother's long blond hair fell gracefully over her shoulder as she tilted her head. She sent Clio an encouraging smile, warming a heart that had iced when Mnemosyne had been mentioned.

"It will work," Zeus announced as he jumped out of his chair. "Until now, the mortals have been attempting to solve the problem with a diplomatic solution." He propped his fingertips on the table and leaned forward. "They do this to avoid warrior action. I've spoken to Mars, and he believes an economic solution might be in order."

All around the table voices rose, a mixture of confusion, excitement, and consternation. Mars offered a solution that was peaceful rather than war-like? Clio wracked her memory. Had anything like this ever happened? She didn't think so.

Polly raised her voice above the others. "The Bringer

of War thinks this can be solved by throwing money at the problem?"

"Yes, and his suggestion makes sense." Zeus skirted the table and strode to Clio's side. He spun her chair until she faced him, and then squatted in front of her. "Daughter, deep within the earth below Bulgaria lies a field of lantern crystals."

"I don't know what those are." Clio held his gaze, knowing he'd tell her in his own good time.

"Lantern crystals are highly conductive rocks, formed in the same manner as diamonds, but they possess a much higher metal content." Zeus's tone was patient. "In Russia, scientists have been seeking an alternative energy source. World-wide consumption is depleting fossil fuels at an alarming rate."

"Okay." Clio dug a little deeper for patience while Zeus meandered through his explanation like it was picnic Sunday at the folly by the pond. The god had spent entirely too much time with Mel lately. Talk about a dramatic reveal.

"This enormous scientific brain trust hypothesizes that connecting a renewable resource, like water or wind, to a conductive substance, like a lantern crystal, will generate inexhaustible power." His look turned triumphant, as if he'd just spelled out something so elementary even a child should understand.

Clio wasn't seeing a solution. "Okay, but how does this impact the challenge?"

Nia fidgeted in her seat. "This is why the Five Nations targeted Bulgaria. They're after the crystal field. If they conquer the country, they'll control the resource. With influence like that, they're in the driver's seat toward resurrecting previous glory. Shoot, they could harness the power of the sun and create weapons of untold power."

Zeus beamed at Nia, pride shining in his eyes. "Correct, my precocious child." He turned his attention back to Clio. "Mars suggests negotiating a trade pact between the Five Nations and Bulgaria. In exchange for full mining rights, the Five Nations will not massacre the native population and will pledge to not use the crystals in the manufacture of weapons. They will also pay the Bulgarian government rent and above average wages to the native citizens working in the mines. Mars also suggests they must make restitution for the lives already forfeited in the wake of their aggression. He'd like to see that paid in the hides of bureaucrats."

Clio allowed hope to rise as she saw the beauty and simplicity of Mars' corporate-esque solution. "Will Bulgaria go for this resolution?"

"I believe this will be something the Muse of History might influence." Zeus patted her knee before pushing to his feet. He rocked back on his heels and crossed his arms over his chest.

Clio searched her memory for situations that might have been similar in history. The closest she could come was the French government and its policy of appeasement during World War Two. They'd given in to German aggression and saved lives. French men and women had survived to fight another day. She'd personally witnessed the efforts of the Resistance fighters.

"This could work." If she managed to convince Jax of the strategy, and he could get the State Department to broker an economic solution, she'd win the challenge and avoid becoming a loathsome bird. Pierus would lose and Tyranny, the bitchy magpie, would be forever caged.

"Oh, and Helios said the Taino storm gods *have* influenced the weather. They've been working overtime from their base in the Dominican Republic to assist Pierus."

"What's in it for them? What could Pierus have offered them to make them act out?" Corie asked, a frown crinkling her pretty brow.

Callie sneered. "Maybe nothing. The lesser gods are

always seeking opportunities to work their magic. Pierus probably told them they could wreak havoc in a couple of places. They'd jump at the chance."

Or it was possible Pierus promised them a larger role in his reimagined corporation once he seized control of Olympus. She sure as hell wasn't letting that happen with her challenge.

Uncertainty had bloomed in her gut with the confirmation that Pierus had teamed up with the mischief-making storm gods. "When we defeat Pierus, we can shut down the weather deities' excess activity and restore order." Clio forced confidence into her voice. She was eager to get on with the task.

"But you must still convince this Jax to help. And his counterparts, who will be descending upon Delphi tomorrow," Gaia said.

Clio was surprised by her mother's words. "What? Who?"

"A veritable army of people from GeoPoly arrives tomorrow. They've reserved the entire resort 'for the duration' I believe were the woman's exact words. She demanded we relocate all of our other paying guests to alternate facilities. The person making the arrangements, a rather pushy woman named Beryl, indicated they would be working closely with your Jax."

"So he's helping *them*." Hurt bloomed, dimming the earlier bright glow of hope. Why hadn't he told her? She dug in her purse for her phone and checked messages. Nothing from him.

Zeus laid his hand on Clio's shoulder as though he knew how much the lack of communication from Jax cut her. "Daughter, the time is drawing near. It appears all players are in place now."

Her heart raced with the idea of the coming battle with this demon. The edges of the phone dug into her palm as she clenched her fist. "I know this is my challenge to face, but I'm glad to have you all behind me. It will be so much easier for us to kick Pierus's ass as a team."

"We will help as we can. Go. Convince your professor to help. This I know you can do." He bent low at the waist and kissed the crown of her head. He straightened and looked at each of his other daughters in turn. "As for the rest of you, your time will come. Watch over Clio, provide support where you can."

They all looked to her. For once, their nudges didn't sting. Positive energy and thoughts rolled off them like fluffy clouds, enveloping her in a warm glow of love. It had been this way for centuries. They banded together to right wrongs and unite their efforts for the good of all mankind. Existing as long as they had was the result of being there for each other. While individually they served to inspire mortals, collectively they joined forces to motivate each other.

Knowing she must face the balance of this challenge with limited direct assistance from her siblings, dread prickled over Clio's scalp and neck. Her sisters would send mental support, but with the vague rules Pierus had thrown out in his e-mail, the daughters of Zeus might only be able to influence mortals unknowingly involved in the challenge. Most likely, they wouldn't be able to do anything to actually help her defeat Pierus's daughter, Tyranny. That sucked monkey balls.

In silence, the girls stood and formed a line behind Zeus, with Gaia at the end. Zeus pressed his forehead to Clio's and whispered his wishes for her success. Clio squeezed her eyes against the emotion threatening to overwhelm. If she failed, this could be the last time she saw him or any of them. He released her and with an optimistic smile left the conference room. Each of her sisters repeated the process until only Thalia and Gaia remained.

Lia laid her forehead on Clio's and whispered a different sort of message. "You seem a little tense, Clio.

You should shag that man of yours. Then you'll be ready to kick Pierus right in the nut sack and show him Muses rule and demi-gods drool. And hit his tyrannical daughter right in the hillbilly. They might have opened Pandora's box, but they'll find nothing but trouble inside. You've got this."

As intended, Lia's words and her easy laughter put a smile on Clio's face. Lia twirled her way out of the room, another maneuver meant to inspire a grin. Deep affection for her goofy sister swirled around Clio's heart. It alleviated the very real pressure that had built in her lungs, making it easier to breathe.

Gaia stroked her hand on Clio's cheek. "You wished to speak to me alone, Clio?"

Clio dragged her gaze from her spinning sister and focused on her mother. "I have a question about something that happened yesterday."

"Let's go sit on the porch swing and enjoy the evening while we talk." Gaia didn't wait for Clio to agree. She simply wrapped her arm around Clio's shoulders and steered her toward the front portico.

Once they'd settled on the glider, Gaia folded her hands in her lap and waited for Clio to speak.

Clio opened her mouth, then snapped it shut again. Seeking the right words, she slumped against the back of the swing and chewed her lower lip.

"Daughter, you're clearly bothered by something. Just say it."

"I think something weird is going on with my gift."

Gaia tipped her head forward and tapped her fingers on her thigh. "What do you mean?"

"Jax seems able to resist my nudges. It's happened more than once, but last night…"

Her mother's fiery blue eyes held the patience of the ages. After a brief pause, she prompted, "Last night?"

"After I told him what I was, he had a lot of questions about stuff that had happened throughout history. I nudged him to get him to stop and listen to what I needed from him, but he kept asking questions." The memory of how her nudge had affected him brought heat to her face. She forged on with her explanation. "He said the touch of my mind to his felt more like a stroke, uh…on a completely different part of his anatomy. Then when I touched his arm and nudged at the same time, he, um, well, let's just say he needed a cold shower."

"I see."

"That's it? I see?" Clio huffed out an exasperated breath and threw herself back against the cushions, stirring the swing to motion. "What does it mean? Is this part of the challenge? Am I losing my powers?"

"Not at all." Gaia patted Clio's knee, then took her hand. Lacing their fingers together, she continued. "Jax's reaction only means he has great affection for you. And you have similar feelings for him. As a Muse, you communicate on a mental level with most people you touch, but you don't know them. With Jax, the communication is more visceral, more physical. True love does this."

"That can't be right. I've been in love before. I've lived for centuries and been married many times. I've never experienced something like this."

"You've never loved like this before."

"I don't know that I love Jax. I barely know him."

Gaia turned in her seat and pressed a finger to Clio's chest. "Your heart knows him. In this lifecycle, you believed you had love for your college sweetheart. A love worthy of binding your life to his for the rest of this lifetime. But I think now you cannot remember his face. That is not true love. For me, I cannot recall his name." Her mother had never liked the man and didn't bother to get to know him while Clio had been dating him.

"His name is Steve. You know that, Gaia."

"Ah, yes. Steve. Did you use your influence with him?

Try to get him to fall in love with you?"

Clio didn't bother to nod. Her mother knew the whole twisted story.

"The touch of your gift didn't affect him the same way as it did with Jax. With Steve," she uttered his name with a sneer, "you nudged him away into the arms of your sorority sister. Because he was not the man you were destined to be with."

"I thought he was." Clio's voice was small as she relived the anguish of Steve's betrayal.

"Your sister, Aerie, would tell you Steve wasn't for you. And she would know."

She rubbed her fist on her sternum, attempting to massage away the remembered sting. "But this doesn't explain why my gift doesn't work the right way with Jax."

"You've met your mortal match." Gaia's smile illuminated the dusk and created warmth in Clio's chest. "In all of your existences, there will be only one man who is affected by your touch in this manner. Only one man whom you will love with every fiber of your being. It appears Jax is that man."

"Well, that's just flipping great. I find the man I'm destined to be with just as I'm about to be turned into a goddamned bird for all eternity."

"Daughter." Gaia's voice was gentling chiding. "The fact that you have found your destiny in Jax feels more like assurance you will succeed in the challenge rather than face defeat. It gives me great hope."

Clio desperately wished it gave her as much hope. Jax still hadn't committed to helping her. As the evening doves cooed in the nearby trees, she examined her heart, her feelings for the man fate had deemed her helper for the challenge Pierus had set. What she found was fear. She was afraid to be with him, afraid he wouldn't help, and then where would she be? But a larger fear sat heavily on her shoulders. The fear of not being with him loomed, a large, frightening blotch of blackness in her life. Her eyes and heart stung with the thought. Like she would step on a bug, she squelched the fright currently trying to steal her breath.

"Will it be this way for all my sisters?" So far in this lifetime, none of them had married.

"That I cannot say. I do not know, but I can dream it will be so. You should all find a love like this once in your existences."

"Like you and Zeus?"

Gaia beamed a smile toward her. "Just like us."

Chapter 14

J ax walked toward her, up the path from the street to his
front door. A slow, sexy smile lit his face. It made her
heart race.

After speaking to Gaia, Clio had driven straight to
Jax's house. Disappointment flattened her spirits when
she'd discovered he wasn't home. But the evening was
pleasant. The sun had begun its final descent behind the
trees and gilded his quiet, residential neighborhood in gold
and pink. The air itself felt charged. Insuppressible hope
tantalized her skin like a lover's touch. If she closed her
eyes, she could pretend it was Jax's hand caressing her
rather than a warm summer breeze.

"Hi," Jax greeted her, his steps scraping against the
cement of the front walk. The sun glinted in his ebony hair,
firing sparks of red and gold on the tips.

He rested one hand on the railing beside her and slid it
forward until he bent enough to capture her mouth.

She let her lips cling to his, open and welcoming.
When he finally broke the kiss, she sighed out a satisfied
breath. "Hi yourself."

He dropped his rump onto the step, crowding in beside
her, thigh to thigh, hip to hip. He leaned his shoulder into
hers. "I'm surprised to see you here."

"Good surprise or bad?"

He leaned away and regarded her for a moment. He
slipped his arm around her shoulders and hugged her close.

"Definitely good." He hit her with a toothy grin. "I was just going to call you."

"Yeah?"

"Yeah. I went out to get a bite to eat with my buddy, Ian. Eating turned into watching a soccer game. Lost track of time." His simple tone and reasonable explanation for his silence today spoke volumes to her soul.

"Jax, I'm sorry to rush you. But I have to know if you're—"

He pressed his fingers against her lips. "Shhh. We'll get to that. Let's just watch the sunset. It's a special one tonight."

Impatience tinted with despair climbed her chest. Why would he stop her words if he didn't mean to help? Her heart grew heavy in the face of his potential rejection. For an instant, she thought to nudge him. Instead, she laid her cheek on his shoulder and joined him in watching the sun disappear in showy hues of orange, red, and indigo. She didn't want this to be her last sunset as a person. But if her fate was sealed, she might as well relish this one glorious moment. The memory was going to have to last an eternity.

As the sun sank from view and rays of fading light struck the clouds, Jax rose. He offered his hand, and when she took it, he pulled her to her feet. Without a word, he led her into the house.

Clio glanced around curiously. Her gaze lit on a massive entertainment center dominating the wall opposite the front door. "Oh, my goddess! Jax, that is the biggest television I've ever seen."

The TV stood in the center of a dark wood unit with ornate crown molding. Shelves filled with electronics, games, and DVD cases surrounded the main attraction. A large sectional sofa faced the unit. The low table in front of it was littered with gaming controls.

Jax looked at it with pride shining in his face. "It's how I relax."

Pulling her hand free, she moved toward the shelves. She trailed her finger over the game cases, reading the titles out loud. *"World of Warcraft, Battlefield, Assassin's Creed. You like your military games, don't you?"*

"Actually, I found those helpful when I studied the implications of a real-world military buildup in an area. It's an underutilized option for understanding the geo-political ramifications of that action." He bent and began stacking the magazines strewn over the table. "The games simulate real world scenarios. It's easy to play my way to reliable predictions for the outcome of armed action."

She glanced over her shoulder. "Plus you like to play them."

Jax stopped tidying and glanced up at her, a crooked smile and devastating dimples on his face. "Yeah. It's fun to blow shit up."

Oh, goddess, those tiny creases on his cheeks did funny things to her insides. With a shaky breath, she faced the shelves again and studied the neatly ordered spines of his collection. She was conscious of his movements behind her.

"Oh, you have my favorite." Clio hooked a finger on the top of the *Call of Duty: Modern Warfare* case and tipped it out. It was the only game she knew of that offered an option of diplomatic resolution in the face of war. Holding it between her thumb and forefinger, she faced Jax. "Want to play?" This would be an excellent way to introduce the idea of the economic solution she had in mind.

"Really? Hell yeah!" Jax lifted one eyebrow. "Want to make it interesting?"

Clio inched her head to the side. "What do you have in mind?"

Moving with predatory grace, Jax stalked to her side. He leaned in, sandwiching her body between him and the entertainment center. Bracing his hands on the shelves behind her, one on each side of her head, he dipped into the crook of her neck. His lips were soft as he nibbled the muscles there. Shivers coursed through her.

"How about strip video game?" He licked his way up to the hollow below her ear. "We play in easy mode." He circled his hips against hers and nipped his way along her jaw. "Loser of each level must remove one article of clothing."

His lips and teeth were magic. Her clothes could melt off under the onslaught of his marauding mouth. She moved her hands to his butt and pulled him closer. It was difficult to catch a breath, let alone speak. "I'm game," she breathed.

Jax smoothed a finger along her collarbone and then curled it under the neck of her T-shirt. Dragging the fabric to one side, he licked the spot he'd just bared and then blew a breath on it before pressing his lips in place. "Winner gets to pick the place, position, and duration of the really awesome sex that will result. Deal?"

Tingles blasted from between her legs, hitting every part of her anatomy. "Deal," she sighed.

The corners of his eyes crinkled with his smile. "A little kiss...to seal the bargain."

He feathered his mouth over hers then pulled her bottom lip between his. Moving her hands up the broad plane of his back, she relished the soft seduction of his mouth and tongue as he deepened the kiss. Screw the video game. Screw her need to get him to help. She just wanted to screw him.

Jax cupped her face between his hands and eased away. Temporarily dazed by the passion in his kiss, Clio blindly followed him as he led her to the couch. He continued to smile at her, as if he knew how he'd affected her. He pushed her down to the cushions, putting her at eye level with his crotch. His cock was firmly outlined behind the zipper of his jeans. Goddess, did she really want to play a game when that waited in his pants for her? She'd caused his bold erection. The knowledge brought a blast of pure pleasure.

Jax snapped his fingers in front of her eyes. She jerked her gaze to his face.

With a smirk, he pushed a controller into her hands. "Ready to lose?"

"Win or lose, doesn't really matter, does it?"

He laughed. "I guess not."

"But, so you know, you're going down."

"Figuratively or literally?"

"Both."

His laughter cracked loudly in the air around her. "God, I need a cold shower after just talking to you. Why don't you go grab us a couple beers from the kitchen while I fire the game up?" Jax picked up a remote and turned on the system, almost as easily as he'd turned her on.

When she returned with two bottles of pale ale, she located coasters and set them down. Reclaiming her seat on the sofa, she squirmed, making herself more comfortable on the soft, buttery leather. The cushions hugged her body like a lover. If she won, she was picking this couch as the scene of her reward. She pulled her feet up and tucked them under her thighs tailor-style. Propping her elbows on her knees, she scrunched over to her favorite gaming position. Jax plopped down right next to her. He grabbed a controller, turned to her, and said, "Let the games begin."

While they played through the first level, it became apparent they were fairly evenly matched. But in a surprise move, Jax surged past her, defeating her strategic play.

"That level to me." He pointed to the table. "Pay up, Clio."

She set her controller on the seat next to her. She snagged the bottom of her navy-blue T-shirt and pulled it over her head, arching her back and jutting her breasts up. Underneath, she wore a snug fuchsia tank top. Holding

Jax's eye, she tossed the scrap of cotton to the center of the table. She pinned him with a look meant to say he wouldn't win the next round. By the sudden gleam in his eyes, she was sure he was determined to defeat her.

They resumed play without a word. This time, Clio set a course toward diplomacy, reserving some of her troops as security forces. Jax deployed his fighters in a blockade around the imaginary nation they fought for. Her strategy would be useful in helping him see a way through the Five Nations situation. She hoped.

While she worked toward the peaceful resolution, she still used her security forces in sniper mode and decimated Jax's army. Level over.

"Damn, you're good at this." Jax's voice was muffled in the dense fabric of his shirt as he pulled it off. Muscles shifted powerfully in his back and abdomen as he leaned forward to drop the shirt on top of hers. "I never saw that coming."

"I'm stealthy that way." She gripped the handles of her controller more firmly. "Round three."

Play continued, each of them getting more intense, more focused on winning the game. For every armed action Jax executed, Clio countered with a reasoned response. She lost the next two rounds. Her bright pink undershirt and her white shorts joined the pile on the table. Jax pressed a kiss to her breast above the black bra she wore. Then he trailed his fingers up her spine, from the elastic lace of her boy-short panties to the nape of her neck.

Using the powerful distraction of her body and a carefully veiled, gentle nudge his direction, Clio won the next round. They were both down to their underwear. Knowing they were so evenly matched, she decided she wasn't above cheating a little. She'd never thought to influence an electronic game, but it was worth a try. She couldn't nudge the game so she turned her gift on herself. Her fingers flew on the controller, defeating Jax's massive troop buildup with diplomacy and an economic resolution. Exactly the same way she hoped to help him resolve the situation in Bulgaria.

The hunk of plastic that had become an extension of his arms as they'd played clunked loudly on the table when Jax tossed it down. "How did you do that? Your solution should never have worked. You obliterated my position without much loss of life and manufactured a…a détente. A diplomatic answer. I'm stunned. I never lose this game."

"Guess you've met your match." Clio dropped her gaze to his green boxers. "I believe the terms were place, position, and duration."

"I believe you are right." His gaze smoldered with desire as he rose from the sofa.

He hooked his hands in the elastic waistband and slid the fabric down his hips and thighs until it settled around his feet. His erection jutted away from his body when he stood straight again. He kicked the boxers away, then stood still waiting for her instruction.

Her heart raced, the pulse pounding in the hollow of her throat. She licked suddenly dry lips. "Here," she said as she uncrossed her legs and spun until her back was against the arm of the couch. She spread her thighs apart, exposing her core to his steamy gaze. "I think you on top, at least to start."

"And duration?" Jax braced one hand on the bolster behind her and leaned down, running the back of his knuckles down the slope of her chest.

She captured his hand and flattened it over her breast, arching into the heat of his palm. "I wouldn't be opposed to all night long, Jax."

Still standing next to the couch, he seized her mouth in a long, drugging kiss. Hooking a hand behind her knee, he jerked her down until she was prone on the soft surface. He pinched his fingers on the front closure of her bra and freed her breasts. He put both hands on them, thumbing her nipples, squeezing gently and circling the areolas. The whole time, he plundered her mouth, stroking his tongue on hers, reaching as far in as possible before retreating, only to thrust again.

He trailed his hands from her breast to her panties. In a smooth motion, he lifted her hips and swept the scrap of lace from her. He tossed it to the pile of clothes on the table.

He pulled his lips from her mouth and kneeled between her legs, his gaze intent on her slit. Reclaiming one breast with his hand, he licked his index and middle fingers. With a wicked grin, he plunged two fingers deep inside her. She gasped then moaned, her hips rocking up, trying to draw his fingers deeper.

"You're already wet for me, Clio." He sucked her nipple between his lips and worked her with deep thrusting motions in her sheath. The rhythm of his mouth matched the motion of his hand, and he pushed her closer and closer to the edge.

Hot, bright sensation grew as he paid attention to all the parts of her anatomy begging for release. Delicious tension spun out of control and crashed over her in a rich splash of color, light, and sensation. She gasped out his name in a quiet squeak that ended on a sigh.

He kissed his way down the center of her body, swirling his tongue in her navel before continuing downward. She pressed her heels against the cushion when he grasped her hips and lifted. He ran his tongue over her slit in a slow, languorous lap. Sparks shot off behind her eyes when he dipped his tongue inside her. He licked, dipped, and nibbled her, building her back to a frenzy.

Unable to bear it any longer, she tangled her fingers in his dark curls and urged him up. But, dear goddess, he took his time. He lowered his chest to the vee of her legs, his hard muscles brushing firmly along her clit as he pushed upward. His erection lay heavily on her thigh. He kissed her belly, then her ribs. His abs flexed against her nub, setting her insides to quaking.

"Jax, please," she begged. She'd expire if he didn't slide into her soon.

"In a minute," he mumbled around a mouthful of her breast.

He rocked his pelvis to her center, making her whimper with need. He repeated the motion until finally the tip of his cock slipped beyond the barrier. He drew back a little farther, then pushed inside, again and again, going a little deeper each time. After minutes of the torture, he thrust hard, groaning as he merged fully with her. Filling her completely.

He reared back and then slammed into her again. Circling his hips, he continued to brush her clit. Waves of pleasure pushed her along a tide so intense it made her heart pound. A spasm began in her center, and her muscles clenched. He turned his face into her neck when she lowered her hand to his ass and clutched him. She matched the movement of his hips, cradling him close, chasing after him. His groans sounded in her ear, his breath hot and moist against her cheek.

Higher and higher he pushed until, like a champagne cork, she burst in a rush of fizzy pleasure. Jax bit the column of her neck as he came, the pain intensely pleasurable. He pounded hard, growling with each thrust. His rhythm slowed, but he continued to strain against her, into her.

Spent, he collapsed on top of her with a rush of breath. "God, Clio!" His voice was like a drug as giddy elation claimed her.

She rested her hands on the curve of his hips and flexed her fingers. She hummed quietly as ripples of aftershocks radiated through her.

Jax lifted his hips slightly, allowing his dick to slip from her body. He settled between her legs again, maintaining skin to skin contact. He cleared his throat, a nervous sound. Opening her eyes, she stared at the ceiling, unsure of what was happening between them.

He rose up on his elbows and gazed at her. "Look at me, Clio." When she did, his brown eyes reflected the light from the television that they'd ignored in the heat of passion. But his emotion was unreadable. "We should talk about the challenge."

Chapter 15

Well, shit. Nerves shot through Jax like a fucking Cupid's arrow. That was never a good way to start a conversation. Clio struggled under him, rocking her hips in an effort to dislodge him from his spot between her legs. A spot he didn't want to relinquish. Ever.

Clio lowered her brow and narrowed her eyes at him. Residual sexual tension stirred his dick. But it wasn't in the same way her mind-meld trick had affected him when she'd nudged thoughts at him. Seeing her squint must have made his cock react like Pavlov's dogs.

"Okay, that came out wrong. I don't mean we should talk, like it's been nice knowing you. But because I have questions."

"Oh." Her voice was uncertain, but hope glimmered in her eyes.

He kissed the tip of her nose. Reaching behind him, he grabbed the blanket draped over the back of the couch. He spread out the fleece, covering them. Not like it was necessary, but because he thought she might be more comfortable not completely exposed to the world. He balanced his weight on his elbows to keep from crushing her.

"I have some questions about you as a Muse."

"I'll answer what I can. But understand, I've never revealed myself this way before. Neither have any of my sisters. This is pretty uncharted territory for us."

"Gotcha." He sucked in a deep breath and asked the question that had bothered him the most. "Are you immortal?"

"My memories are immortal. But physically I'm mortal."

"Explain."

"I have a life span, just like a normal human. I'm born, I age…I die." She toyed with a bit of fringe on the blanket. "My body exists on this mortal plane. My memories exist in Olympus."

"Hang on! Olympus is real?"

She laughed. "Yes. It exists just beyond the veil of ether surrounding the earth. You can't actually see it, but you can sense it. In those moments of déjà vu common among humans, you catch glimpses of it. But for the last two hundred years, it's been run as a multinational corporation."

"Sweet. We'll get back to that. Okay, keep going. What happens to the memories once your body dies?"

"When I'm reborn, I come with all the accumulated memories of our entire life experience." She sighed, her breath warm on his cheek. "Same for my sisters. We remember everything, which makes our jobs easier. None of us come into our gifts right away. We live in a period of dormancy when we can't impact the world."

"So you're all born and die at the same time?"

"Goddess, no! My poor mother couldn't handle a litter of nine. No woman could. We really are as mortals. Although I do have twin sisters." Her smile was sweet as she talked about her sisters. "They are a matched set and always come together. But we come into our powers individually, even them. And we die separately."

"What happens to the rest of humanity during your dormant period?"

"Depends. Bloody Mary Tudor sat on the throne of England one time. The Dark Ages were the longest periods.

Our life spans weren't as long then. Our worst time was during the bubonic plague. Had our powers not been dormant, we'd have found a way to influence world leaders to implement better sanitation." She frowned. "Oh, and the Spanish Inquisition. By the time our powers emerged in the sixteenth century, the inquisition had been going strong. It's hard to combat religious zealots. We'd just about get it under control, then we'd die. Life spans weren't as long back then, you know. By the time we came into our powers again, the brutal Inquisition was back in full swing. It took a long time to fix that."

Jax toyed with the strap of the bra he'd opened, but they hadn't managed to remove. The ages when the world seemed dim suddenly became a little clearer in his mind. "That explains a lot. Remind me to ask you about Napoleon sometime."

"Okay. But you should know he was actually compensating for his height by trying to conquer the world."

He laughed. The muscles in his shoulders were twitching, so he rolled off Clio and nestled in next to her. He tucked the blanket under her hip then rested his hand on her flat belly. "How did you figure out using a diplomatic solution on the game? I've played that way, but diplomacy almost never works."

A becoming pink color washed her cheeks. "Um, I might have cheated a little."

"You mean like you used your power on it? You can cheat an inanimate object like that?" Incredible if it was true.

She grinned at him. "Not on the game. But I gave myself a nudge to work faster to find the hole in your strategy. It worked."

He remained silent for a moment, contemplating her resolution. A light popped in the corner of his mind. Hers had been a sound approach. It made him think of the situation in Bulgaria. He struggled to not get his hopes up for a similar peaceful resolution overseas. "Is there a hole in the Five Nations plan?" If anyone knew, it would be Clio.

She rolled on her side to face him and lifted her thigh over his. "Yes, we believe we've found a workable option to circumvent further bloodshed."

"We? Your sisters and you?"

"My parents helped, too."

"Your dad, Zeus, right? King of gods?"

She grimaced. "Yeah. Zeus and Gaia."

Jax snorted. "Of course. I'm not much on mythology, but I believe that."

"Jax, we can stop the Five Nations aggression." She shoved up on her elbow until she was face-to-face with him, her blue eyes electrified by some glow from within. "We believe their motivation is greed. Bulgaria has something they want. Beneath their soil is a vast field of crystals. According to Mars, the Bul—"

"Mars? Like God of War Mars?"

"Yeah. He's my uncle."

Jax groaned out a laugh and slid onto his back. He clutched her hips and urged her to straddle him.

After shedding her bra, she propped her forearms onto his chest. The points at which the taut nubs of her nipples pressed against his chest distracted him. Shit, he had to focus. He sent his dick an at-ease command and was relieved when it sort of listened.

She regarded him earnestly. "Anyway, according to Mars, the Five Nations need these crystals as an energy resource. Pierus is exploiting the situation of the five governments to help free his daughters and take over my father's corporation. We believe he thinks your lack of success in the region previously would render it difficult for you to embrace the *what if* this time around. We disagree."

She outlined a plan for a peaceful end to the conflict using economic motivation as the catalyst. Jax tightened his fingers on her hips as she spoke. Her plan should work.

Would work.

"Clio, you might just have spared humanity the terror of World War Three." He grasped her shoulders and pulled her against his chest, claiming her mouth with a fast, hard kiss. This time, he could make a difference.

"Gaia said your people from GeoPoly are arriving tomorrow. Does this mean you'll help?"

"What are the chances the plan could backfire because you used magic to manufacture an end to the Five Nations assault?"

"But I didn't. When we discovered what my nudges did to you, I decided we needed a non-magic solution. You had to focus on the problem, not on how desperate you were to make love to me. Or how frantic I was to have you do that." She swept her fingers through his hair, pushing the longer ends on the crown of his head backward. "This solution is one hundred percent not magic. And it will work."

"I'm in. I was going to help you all along. First, because you are right. I am desperate to join with you, to move over you and in you every moment we are together." His dick jumped in agreement. She wiggled her bottom over the sudden stiffness prodding her backside. His breath stuttered, but he forced himself to continue. "But secondly, I figured maybe with you by my side, I might be able to get my former employer and the government to listen. Can you prod them to do what we need them to?"

"Absolutely."

"Good." Her skin was like silk as he smoothed his hands up her arms. "My former boss, Beryl, has made arrangements for us to use one of the private meeting rooms at the library for the duration. We needed a spot big enough to accommodate a good number of people and one with access to a network. She's greased the wheels with the university and the library director."

"That's good. I'll be close if you need me to push anyone."

One more fear surfaced, a feeling so strong it nearly stole his breath. "Will winning this conflict mean you defeat Pierus's challenge? Now that I've found you, I don't want to let you go."

"Since I'm the first of my sisters that he's challenged…" She bit her lip and glanced away. "Jax, we don't know. We think yes. History has taught us to be vigilant when it comes to him. This dispute with Pierus goes back to the fifth century BC. He surfaces ever few thousand years to try to free his children. But, this is the first time the tests are to be faced individually. We won't know what other tricks he has in store for us. Even if I win, if one of my sisters loses, we all lose."

"Nope. I'm not going to spend the rest of my life with you as a bird. That just doesn't work into my plans."

A slow smile spread over her lovely face. "The rest of your life?"

"Yeah. That doesn't scare you, does it?" It should have scared the shit out of him to think about growing old with a goddess…wife…by his side. But he searched deep within and found only excitement about the possibility.

She shook her head as she lowered her mouth to his. Just before she touched his lips with hers, she breathed against them. "Not in the least, my love. Not in the very least."

* * *

Clio spent the night in Jax's arms in his bed. It was the best sleep she'd gotten since learning of the challenge. The normally enchanting alarm on her phone beeped harshly before the sun came up, and she snoozed it, not wishing to leave the cocooning warmth of Jax's magnificent body. When it went off a second time, she reluctantly rose. A small thrill went through her when a bare-chested Jax walked with her to where she'd left her car parked at the curb.

The sky blazed red and orange as the sun rose on the eastern horizon. Clouds churned ominously in the west. By the time she arrived at her tiny house, the fiery colors had faded to iron gray. Her spirits sank like a rock in a pond. The storm was definitely coming today. Would this be her last sunrise?

As she walked up the steps to her home, a magpie cackled from its perch on the corner street sign. Clio paused to glare at the bird. "You won't win. I will defeat you," she whispered. The black and white monstrosity lifted its wings, as though shrugging, dismissing her words.

Clio let herself into the house. She stopped in the kitchen to start coffee before heading to the shower. Thirty minutes later, she stood in her bathrobe, mug in hand, staring into her closet. She'd be meeting Jax's former co-workers today. Possibly helping them save the world. Definitely saving her own life. She slid a couple of hangers to the side and pulled her favorite scarlet top from the rod, then reached back in for the comfortable black pants suit she considered her VIP visitor outfit. She straightened her hair until it hung sleek and smooth against her jaw, spraying it with more than enough product to maintain the style.

She was startled to hear humming as she walked to the kitchen for a refill. She slowed her step and with her free hand dug through her purse looking for her pepper spray. She might be a Muse, able to influence people to do what she willed, but sometimes a girl just had to rely on more mortal options. A nudge from her, plus a jet of burning hot liquid in the face, was guaranteed to work wonders.

"Come in. I've made you breakfast."

Relief trickled down her spine at the sound of her father's voice. She dropped the small canister of spray back into her bag. "Zeus, what are you doing here?"

He glanced over his shoulder but continued to drizzle amber-red honey into a bowl of yogurt. He lifted one brow. "Is there some law that says I cannot have breakfast with my daughter occasionally?"

She shook her head. "No, but normally you call first. And what the hell are you wearing?"

She'd never understand her father's sense of style. Today he had on his ceremonial toga but had draped it with a tartan plaid sash. On his feet, he wore a beat-up pair of red Chuck Taylor sneakers.

"You mother wondered as well. She threatened to forbid me to leave. But I like to be comfortable." He picked up a small bowl filled with dried fruit and chopped nuts and sprinkled the contents over the creamy white yogurt. He'd fixed a second bowl for himself. Clio grabbed another mug from the cabinet and poured her favorite hazelnut coffee into it, then topped hers off. Carrying both mugs, she joined Zeus at the table.

While Zeus doctored his drink with cream and sugar, she swirled her spoon in the bowl, mixing all the ingredients together. She took a bite and savored the sweet-tart taste on her tongue. "Oh, you added cinnamon. It's good."

Zeus slurped his coffee. He gazed at Clio as she ate, the expression on his face sober.

"Dammit, Zeus. You are not here for a normal breakfast. You're here because you think it might be the last time you'll see me," she accused.

"I will not deny this thought crossed my mind, daughter." Zeus crossed his arms over his chest and slid lower in his chair, legs spread wide. "But I am feeling confident in our proposed solution. I believe you will win this challenge."

"Then you'll have to sit through eight more daughters facing the same thing." Appetite suddenly gone, Clio let her spoon plop into the bowl.

"We cannot know what they will face, but if we meet it together, as a family, our chances increase of pulling off the ultimate victory."

"I'm scared, Zeus. What if Jax can't convince his boss to pursue the option we came up with? What if she's immune to the power of my nudges? What if they fail and war erupts in Europe?" Fear sat like a stone on her chest. The few bites of food she'd eaten roiled in her stomach. "I don't want to turn into a stinking bird for all eternity, but I'm more concerned about the potential loss of life. And the future of the human race."

"The challenge required that you get the man helping you to entertain the magic of *what if*. Jax has agreed to help, correct?"

She nodded.

"And he believes in your magic, correct?"

She nodded again.

"Then I think you have already won the competition. Saving the world is just like the topping on your yogurt." He pointed to her bowl. "A bonus."

But had she done enough? Jax was willing to help. He'd embraced the idea of her being a Muse. He had to believe in magic for that to happen.

Clio ran a finger over the rim of her mug. "His people are arriving today. He told me they'd reserved a meeting room at the library, so I'll be available to help if needed. He doesn't want me turned into a bird either."

"Of all of Pierus's horrible daughters, Tyranny is the worst. For generations, humans accused me of being tyrannical. I am not even close. If she is released, I fear for the mortals we have loved and guided for the millennia." He sat forward and cupped her face. His cobalt eyes burned with sincere flame. "So, darling daughter, please do your best to see to Jax's success. Gaia and I will be near if you need us. Our laws ensure we can't interfere with the humans involved, but we can advise you. And my advice is try your very hardest."

Chapter 16

W hen Clio entered her office a short while later, the ugly bird perched in the bushes just outside her window. After dropping her purse and insulated mug, she crossed to the window, wildly waving her arms in the air, hoping to frighten the magpie away. Damn thing blinked a human-looking blue eye and flapped its wings, but didn't launch into the air. The top of its wings were bare of feathers. Bone and sinew ended in small, fingerlike protrusions on the tips. Was the magpie so close to success that it was transforming back to a person?

Disgusted and worried, Clio seized the string tie of the blinds and jerked it to the left. The thin wooden planks clacked as they fell into place. Then she twisted the slats closed, blocking out the sight of the evil Tyranny. Feeling defiant, Clio lifted her middle finger in the bird's direction.

She turned her back to the window. A glance at the ormolu clock with the delicate cherub sitting atop showed Clio had an hour before Jax and his crew arrived. The facilities director would have already taken care of setting up the room they'd reserved. She sat down to concentrate on her e-mails and work on her departmental budget. Although, she wondered why she bothered. They couldn't fire her if she was a magpie.

The office remained quiet except for the ticking clock and Tyranny's occasional aggravating squawk. When the phone on the corner of the desk buzzed, it startled her. Her phone almost never rang.

Heart racing, she answered. "Hello?"

"Clio, it's Zeke."

"What are you doing here this morning?" He typically worked at night. It was unusual for him to be in the library at nine in the morning.

"Regular guy called off sick. Professor Callahan is at the front desk. And he has a rather large contingent of people with him."

"Would you mind directing them to the Ancient Civ room. I'll join them there."

"Sure thing." Zeke hung up before Clio could utter her thanks.

She gave them thirty minutes to settle in before going to greet the visitors. After a stop in the employee break room for a refill, she headed to meet Jax and his co-workers.

A sign outside the space indicated the room was reserved for the next week and apologized for the inconvenience. It also directed any readers to take their questions directly to Clio. She supposed that was fair, since it was her particular department that was being affected.

Beneath her fingers the brass doorknob was as cold as the dread in her soul. The normally quiet room was abuzz with activity and a loud hum of many voices. Every available surface had notepads, tablets, laptops and wires strewn over it. Cables snaked from the dropped ceiling, and in one corner, a man with a tool belt stood on the highest rung of a stepladder, the top half of his body disappearing into an opening in the fiberglass panels.

Clio scanned the room for Jax. She stopped moving forward when she spied him standing near a table across the room. The look on his face was stormy and grim.

His shoulder appeared stiff under the proprietary hand of a gorgeous blonde. Her candy-apple red nails stood out against the stark white of Jax's button down shirt. The woman's breast brushed Jax's bicep as she pointed to something on the paper he held. Jealousy rose like black, oily smoke in Clio's chest. Fighting the urge to streak across the room and scratch the woman's eyes out, she curled her fingers and dug her own unpainted nails into the palm of her hand.

Jax looked up and met Clio's gaze. His expression immediately lightened. His lips lifted in the slow, sexy smile she'd come to adore above all his other expressions. He shifted away from the blonde and beckoned Clio to his side.

He greeted her with a kiss, smoothing his hand down her arm. "Clio Thanos, this is Beryl Ramsey. Beryl, Clio is the director of the Civilizations Division here in the University Library."

Clio faced Beryl and stifled a shiver produced by the frosty look on the woman's face. Schooling her own face into a placid expression, she extended her hand. "Pleased to meet you, Beryl. Welcome to Delphi."

Beryl curled her lips up in a snarky smile as she gave Clio the once-over that seemed to find her lacking. "Thank you." Clio found her hand engulfed in the woman's hard, cold mitt.

When Beryl released her grip, Clio shoved her fist behind her back and flexed her fingers, hoping to ease the sting of Beryl's crushing greeting. Clio glanced around the room. "Looks like you are getting everything in place. Is there anything you need?"

Leaning his chest into her shoulder, Jax scooted closer to Clio. He grasped her sore hand and massaged it. "I think we're all set. Beryl and the rest of the crew arrived early this morning and, as you can see, they've been hard at work."

"Actually, Jax, I do need one thing," Beryl cooed. "Would you mind if I sleep with you? At your house? My hotel room is hideous. I doubt I'll be able to sleep there."

Bitch tried to intimidate her, and now she was dissing

Clio's parents' resort. There wasn't a single hideous room in the entire inventory of twenty spacious suites. To make matters worse, she wanted to sleep with Jax. Clio turned a cold stare on Jax to see how he'd respond to Beryl's request.

"I'll have plenty of room at my house." Son of a— He'd welcome this—this awful, aggressive woman into the bed Clio had slept in last night. He slipped his hand into Clio's and laced his fingers between hers. "I'll be staying at Clio's house, so feel free to make yourself at home in mine."

Clio's spirits soared.

Beryl's brows lowered in a thunderous scowl. She crossed her arms over her ample chest and shifted her weight to one hip. "We'd better get back to work. The threat from the Five Nations is escalating, and standing around talking isn't going to solve the problem. Admiral Burton from the Joint Chiefs is demanding a military action plan today. I'm sure you'll excuse us, Clio." Beryl pivoted on one stiletto heel but spun back around quickly. "Oh, we could use coffee. Can you make that happen?" She sent Clio a derisive sneer, the kind normally reserved by haughty generals when dealing with enlisted men. Without waiting for an answer, Beryl strode away, hips swishing from side-to-side.

For some people there simply was no excuse. Clio wanted to shout that she'd be happy to pick up the admiral's name after the bitch had dropped it so carelessly. Burton might be one of the highest-ranking military officers now, but he amounted to chump change in Clio's world. Wouldn't it surprise Beryl to know that in the late eighteenth century, Clio had not only known Admiral Horatio Nelson, but had introduced the inspirational British leader to his wife?

Jax jiggled her hand and gave her a tight smile. His soft brown eyes went hard when he looked at Beryl as she stopped to berate one of the techs. He shook his head. "Sorry about that."

"What is she to you, Jax?"

"It's what she used to be and never will be again." He sighed, grasped her shoulders, and urged her to face him. "I've worked with Beryl since I took the position with GeoPoly. She's been my boss and my lover. And she was never good at either role."

"Oh."

"Clio, you have nothing to worry about with her. Is it okay if I stay with you?"

The tension in Clio's neck and shoulders eased. "Sure. But for the record? There are no hideous rooms at the Athenian. My parents own it, and it is charming and five-star all the way."

"I believe you." He pressed a gentle kiss to her cheek.

Across the room, Beryl watched, her lips pursed. Clio summoned every bit of her willpower to stop herself from fondling Jax's luscious ass. But she did nudge Beryl to look away and was pleased when the woman complied. Clio directed her attention back to Jax.

The man watched her with a knowing smile. "I like that you are jealous."

"I'm not. I'm not jealous," Clio insisted. She lowered her voice further. "But I should let you get back to work. Have you talked to her about our idea?"

"There hasn't been time yet. She's been too busy throwing her weight around."

"Holy shit!" A man seated in front of one of the laptops shouted. "Beryl, you better come look."

Clio rested her hand on Jax's arm. "Uh-oh. Sounds like something is happening. You'd better get back to work. Text me if you need me to throw *my* weight around."

Jax captured her mouth under his in a fast urgent kiss. "Don't get too far away, okay? I don't want to lose track of you."

"I'll be in my office on the third floor or at the front desk. I'll let you know if I'm going anywhere else."

Jax nodded, then hurried across the room toward where Beryl and several other people had clustered around a computer.

Clio eased the door shut behind her and strolled down the hall, her heels clacking against the marble floor. When she was almost back to her office, her phone vibrated. She pulled it out and glanced at the screen. Shaking her head, she answered, forcing energy and enthusiasm into her tone. "Hi, Callie." Her sister used to be happier in other lifetimes. For some reason, she acted as if she had her thong underwear on backward this entire existence.

"Have you heard what's going on over there? The Five Nations Block is marching on Sofia."

Damn, this was not good. "Jax and his people are on it. I just left them."

"Are you okay?" Was that actually concern in Callie's voice?

Lightning flashed in the oriel window near the top of the wide staircase. Clio gripped the stone railing but continued up. Fat raindrops pelted the window, creating a racket in the echoing stairwell.

Clio wasn't going to let the rain scare her, even though the gathering storm made her insides quake. She shoved the trepidation lingering at the base of her neck as far away as she could. "It's not over yet, Callie. I'm fine. I'll be fine."

"I know I haven't been very nice lately, Clio. I'm sorry. For all the times I've been mean or bossy or downright nasty to you."

"Callie, you don't have to apologize. Nothing is going to happen to me. You'll have an opportunity to be hateful to me for a long time."

That got the smallest laugh out of her sister. "Please be careful, Clio. I don't want to lose you."

"I love you, Callie."

Callie rang off after muttering she loved Clio as well. A cold corner of her heart thawed with her sister's sentiment.

She settled behind her desk and opened the Internet. The news sites were ablaze with breaking stories, each one reported in the most sensational way possible. The faux sincerity in the reporters' voices grated like sandpaper. She shut down the browser in disgust and focused on library business. An hour passed before the need for more coffee drove her away from her desk.

As she headed toward the first floor break room where they had a better coffee station, she had to pass the Ancient Civ room. The door was cracked open, and she paused. Voices engaged in heated argument filtered out. She made out Jax's low tone, edged with anger and frustration. A woman answered in a strident voice, her words coming too fast for Clio to make much sense of them. Sharp words, accompanied by heel-clacking footsteps, drew closer to where Clio stood in the hall. The door slammed closed, shutting off any further eavesdropping. With a silent prayer for Jax's good luck in convincing Beryl of the strength of their plan, Clio continued on her way.

As she left the kitchen, Clio noticed Zeke seated at the front desk. His two-way radio rested on the counter next to him, and he'd hunkered down on the high stool facing the entry. One elbow propped next to the ID scanner, his chin resting in his hand, he stared at the windows on his right.

Clio scanned her badge and slipped beyond the gate. "Zeke, where's the student scheduled to work this station today?"

"That wuss? The storm shook him like a nut from a tree. I sent him to help shelve books deep in the confines, away from any windows. He promised to be back in time for me to do the security round at eleven."

"I can stay here if you have something to do."

"You are welcome to keep me company, but I'm good

for a little while." He patted the stool next to him.

"I have a few minutes." Clio set her travel mug down and swung the stool around. She slipped onto it as Zeke checked in a dripping student.

"Jeez, it's like the weather gods are pissed off about something. I can't remember the last time it rained this much in the summer." Zeke's conversational tone was at odds with the serious expression in his eyes.

Yeah, there was something supernatural afoot for real. Before she could answer, lightning blazed, the brilliance and violence of the flash temporarily blinding Clio. She lifted her shoulders to wait for the corresponding thunder. The mouse rattled on the counter as the sonic boom rumbled for what seemed like an eternity.

Zeke cleared his throat and twisted to face her. "Clio, I probably should have told you this sooner, but it's not coincidence I'm here today. Your dad—"

The door banged open, and the entering student turned until he faced outside. Standing transfixed, he held the door, as if he wanted to slam it shut but was paralyzed. The hair on Clio's arms rose, and she was instantly alert. She sent a nudge to the student that he wanted to close the storm out. The kid jumped and swung shut the door with another loud bang. He stumbled backward then turned and hurried toward where she and Zeke were seated.

Clio recognized the kid's shaggy multicolored hair. Brian shook excess water away as he scanned in his student ID. "There's a flock of the biggest birds I've ever seen in the bushes outside the door. They are squawking up a storm. I thought birds shut up in storms."

Clio's heart stuttered. "A flock of birds?"

"Yeah, there must a good dozen of them. Big, messy black-and-white fuckers. Sorry."

The security gate unlocked with a click. After a quick glance over his shoulder, shaggy Brian shoved the wooden panel open. His tennis shoes squeaked on the stone floor as he hustled away.

Clio stood and stared at the door, indecision churning in her gut. If all the sisters were gathered, it must be time for the main event. Sharp, gripping pain stabbed her neck. She cried out and grabbed the back of the chair.

"Clio?" Zeke's voice was muffled, as if coming through pea-soup fog.

The lights on the ornate chandelier over the desk flickered and dimmed. Or maybe it was just her vision. Some unseen force compelled her to move forward, and nothing she did to combat the pressure worked to stop her forward motion. She darted her eyes to Zeke and tried to speak, but no words came out.

Zeke slipped off his stool, grabbed her arm, and jerked her backward. He shook her. "Clio! Snap out of it."

She tried to grab his hand as she slid through the gate. The grip on her lessened a little and behind her, Zeke gasped, bending double and clutching his head.

Oh shit. Whoever was trying to control her had attacked Zeke. She reared back to break free of the supernatural grip as Zeke groaned and plunged to his knees. Immediately, tension returned to her neck, and she felt herself being compelled toward the door. She couldn't command her muscles to resist or find her voice to scream for help. Clio blasted a frantic nudge toward Jax, not at all certain it would reach him while she was being controlled by another power.

The door swung open ahead of her, and she was drawn inexorably toward it. Her feet floated an inch above the floor. Pierus stood just beyond the portico. When lightning flashed, his shadow splashed grotesquely misshapen, bulbous, and writhing across the marble floor.

Fighting the constriction gripping her body, she concentrated on grabbing the doorjamb as she was forced over the threshold. Her fingers twitched ineffectually. Knifelike pain screamed through her body as she passed through the doorway. When she'd cleared the edge of the overhanging roof, water cascaded down her face. Magpies cackled, then swooped and swirled. The pressure changed around her body when the birds spun around her like a tornado. Feathers brushed her face, and one bird's finger-like nubs raked her arm. As Clio stood spellbound, the bird's beak transformed to a nose and most of the feathers melted away to reveal a human face. Spiky pinfeathers stuck up on the crown of the head like a wild headdress.

"Clio!"

She struggled against the intense pressure holding her in place and twisted until she looked over her shoulder. Zeke stood in the library entrance, arms outstretched, strain and fright on his face. Some unseen force flung him backward and slammed the door shut.

All around her, thunder boomed, sounding suspiciously like maniacal laughter. Oh, goddess, this was it. She'd convinced Jax to believe in her but he hadn't been able to make the awful Beryl listen to him. She'd lost and was going to become a magpie. Hot tears mingled with the cold rain on her face. Wind buffeted her and her body grew heavier. Her heart seemed the only muscle capable of movement, and it galloped until it felt ready to burst.

Terror and anguish burgeoned in her chest, crowding out all other thoughts. This might be her last moment as a Muse. Thousands of years spent guiding and helping mankind was coming to an end. The world would be a bleak, dreadful place without the Muses inspiring people to achieve greatness with art, music, science, and the rest of their gifts. She'd never see her parents or sisters again. She wasn't going to live happily ever after with Jax.

Feathers flailed against her, and the horrifying fingers scraped her arms. The world plunged into a void as though all air had been sucked from the atmosphere. Thunder boomed one final time, and her world faded to gray.

Chapter 17

J ax whipped his head up when, in the midst of an insane argument with Beryl, his dick turned to steel. What little blood remained north of the button on his jeans flashed hotly into his cheeks. It felt as if Clio had nudged him. He spun around, seeking her presence in the room. Worry replaced desire when he failed to locate her.

As the storm reached its zenith, every computer flickered and dimmed. Beryl's eyes were flinty as she screamed for one of the techs to restore power to the network.

Footsteps pounded down the hall, clearly audible in the enclosed space. The door crashed open and a hulk of a man careened past the threshold. Water dripped off his closely cropped blond hair. His security guard uniform shirt was plastered over his bulky muscles.

The man swept a frantic gaze around the room then finally lit on Jax. He jabbed a finger at him. "I need to speak to you immediately."

Recognizing the panicked man as the fellow who checked him in after hours, Jax took a step toward him.

"Stop right there, Jax." Beryl's strident voice raked against his eardrums. "We're not finished here."

Flashing his hand up in Beryl's face, Jax attempted to force into his voice a calm he didn't feel. "We're not doing anything except waiting for a response from the admiral. I'll be right back."

He hurried over to the guard's side. "Zeke, right?"

"Yeah. It's Clio." Zeke shot a cautionary look in Beryl's direction, then shook his head. He motioned to the hall. "Not here."

He spun around and bustled out the door. Jax followed closely on his heels as the man sprinted up the steps. Together they pounded down the hall. They entered a small private office. The nameplate on the desk declared it Clio's.

"What's going on?" The worry that had burst into Jax's chest when Zeke had arrived had grown until simple inhalation was painful.

The frosted glass in the door rattled when Zeke shoved it closed. He held up a hand, stalling Jax's questions. Dropping his head back, the guard closed his eyes, his lips moved soundlessly. A solid ache built behind Jax's eyes as he waited for whatever the man would reveal.

Zeke opened his eyes and pinned his gaze on Jax. "I know you know what Clio is. What she's dealing with. You're supposed to be helping her. She's been taken."

"What do you mean? Who's taken her?"

"That cocksucker, Pierus."

"Goddammit! We have to get her back."

"We're on it." Zeke's shoulders lifted as he sucked in a deep breath. "Prepare yourself. You're about to meet Clio's dad, Zeus. And he ain't happy."

The atmosphere in the small office suddenly changed, like the air in the room grew dense around his body. Congestion built in Jax's ears as if he was in an unpressurized airplane. He swallowed hard, but the crushing weight in his head didn't diminish. Zeke gripped Jax's shoulder between his thumb and forefinger and dug in as a loud crack sounded, followed by a sharp ozone scent.

"Sorry, it sucks for mortals when gods pop in like this." Zeke eased his grip on Jax, but spun him until he faced the opposite direction. There had just been two of them in the office when they'd entered. Now a third man stood with them.

The newcomer appeared middle-aged. Gray at the temples peppered the jet-black waves cascading around the man's clean-shaven face. A scowl pulled the man's brows together, his lips pursed and echoing the symmetry of the straight, angry line on the man's forehead. And holy shit, was he wearing a toga?

With barely a glance at Jax, the man pinned Zeke with a glare. "Report." As he barked the command, the man's voice echoed eerily in the room.

Zeke went down on one knee, his face averted. "Pierus and his skanky brats compelled Clio beyond the secured perimeter we created. Once she crossed the barrier, they swarmed her. By the time I made it to the door, they'd lifted her in the air and just vanished." He raised his gaze, sorrow, anger, and worry swimming in his eyes. "I've failed. I am sorry, Zeus."

"We did the best we could to see to her safety. Pierus was simply better than us. This time." Zeus turned his attention to Jax. He extended his arm to him, clasping his powerful hand around Jax's forearm, gladiator style. "You are Jax. Nice to meet you, son."

"Where have they taken Clio?"

Zeus relaxed his grip but didn't remove his hand from Jax's arm. "We are not sure. We are sending trackers out, but we need a general location to start. We will find her before it's too late. Have you made any inroads with the Five Nations?"

"Unfortunately, progress is slow. Admiral Burton isn't buying the idea that they'd be satisfied with being able to mine the crystal field." Jax rubbed his hand on the back of his neck. "Hell, he doesn't even believe there *is* a crystal field."

"What would persuade him?"

"A geological report would be best. I've been searching for some intel even hinting at its existence. But the Bulgarians have hidden any mention of this asset too well. I haven't found a damn thing yet. We have to rescue Clio."

"First things first. Our best recourse to reclaim my daughter is to achieve success on the Eastern European front." Zeus crossed his arms over his chest and squeezed his eyes shut.

Jax shot a glance to Zeke who stood with his hands clasped behind his back. He reminded Jax of one of the queen's guards. "What's he doing?"

"He's talking to one of the other gods." Zeke kept his voice low and controlled.

"Are you one of them? One of the gods? Clio didn't mention you."

"No, I'm merely a servant. And Clio doesn't know. I'm kind of undercover. I've been in Clio's life in one form or another since men stopped believing in the existence of immortals."

"Why doesn't she recognize you?" Jax eyed Zeus as he held a mute conversation.

"Did she explain about her living and dying as a mortal?"

"Yeah, she mentioned it." God, what was taking Zeus so long? Clio could be anywhere and in dire straits. The idea that she was already transformed to a bird made him dizzy. Sucking in a deep breath, he bent and propped his hands on his knees. Struggling for calm, he focused his attention on what Zeke was saying.

"My existence is tied to hers. When she passes, I do as well. When she is reborn, I come back also. But where her form rarely changes, mine does. So she never recognizes me from one lifetime to the next. Zeus sent me back as a Great Dane once."

"Jax." Zeus's voice rang with triumph. "Gaia has created the report you require and uploaded it to one of GeoPoly's servers. She tells me she inserted it into a topographic survey of the area. Are you familiar with the file?"

Jax straightened. It shouldn't surprise him that they'd have access to the secured servers. They were Greek gods, after all. But he'd never thought of them in present day terms. In his mind they drove chariots, not cars, and communicated through oracles, not cellphones and e-mail.

He forced his attention back to the man in front of him. "Yes. But what about Clio?"

Zeus's expression softened slightly. "Give me your cellphone number. I will text you the instant we know anything. For now, we need you to defeat the challenge by ending the threat from the Five Nations."

"If the report is there, I can convince the admiral. As soon as he's on board, he'll get the State department involved. Might be a few hours."

"We should know where Clio is by then." Zeus clasped Jax's forearm. "You go do what you need to do to make sure Clio stays a Muse. Your Earth will be a horrible place to exist if we fail."

The air compressed around Jax again as the most badass of all the gods blinked out of the room. Jax's ears popped, and he shuddered.

"Let's go." Zeke motioned toward the door. "We need a cover for me so I can stay in the Ancient Civ room with you. I'll be staying with you as a conduit to communicate with Zeus as soon as you make some progress."

"Shouldn't you be helping in the search for Clio? Can't I just text him?"

"Did he give you his number?"

"No."

"Then I stay. I'm the only way you'll be able to reach him."

Together, they jogged back to the second floor. On the way, Jax considered what story he'd use to explain Zeke's presence. "How are you at flirting?" he asked as they sped down the hall.

"I can give Cupid a run for his money."

"Good. I'm going to introduce you as my grad assistant. I want you to blow as much smoke up Beryl Ramsey's ass as possible. I'm just going to apologize right now. Saves time later." He slowed to a stop just outside the door. Clio had been gone at least fifteen minutes. In the political game of cat and mouse, that was a lifetime. Each minute that passed put her in further danger. He faced Zeke. "Promise me Zeus and his trackers will locate her. And I want to be there when we go get her."

"I can't promise that, man. Remember, I'm just a servant. But I'll do what I can."

Jax took a calming breath, knowing he'd have to locate the report Gaia had planted for them. That report was the only thing standing between success and World War Three. And between Clio and an eternity spent as a magpie.

He could not...would not allow Pierus to triumph.

* * *

The flickering behind Clio's eyelids forced her back to consciousness. She struggled to open her eyes, but it felt as though they were weighed down by the coins Charon placed on the face of the newly deceased as he ferried them across the River Styx. Her chest ached and her head pounded. And the stench was overpowering. Somewhere near she heard muttering and whispering but she failed to make out any words as she slid back into the arms of Morpheus.

When next she awoke, the muttering was absent and the pain in her head had lessened. Laying prone on a very hard surface, she opened her eyes. She didn't move as she tried to sense any other presence in the area. When she didn't detect any other beings, god, mortal, or animal, she lifted her head to look around the dimly lit space.

Oh, goddess! They'd put her in an oversized, gilded cage. On her right, there was a crusty perch suspended from the bars overhead. It smelled worse than the chicken coop at the French farm where they'd lived during the persecution of the Huguenots. In one corner stood a plain metal bucket.

Clio strained to see into the gloom beyond the pen. She could barely make out the craggy ceiling of some kind of cavern. The dull charcoal-colored stone that formed the roof reminded her of the granite mined in Corfu for many years. The air was damp against her skin and a muted roar, like the steady assault of waves, made her wonder if she was near an ocean.

Rolling to her side, she swept her gaze around the grotto seeking any signs of life. In one corner a dead tree with twisted, barren branches stood in a patch of sandy soil. She counted nine limbs climbing upward. She pushed upright and clasped her arms around her legs.

She was in Pierus's lair, wherever that might be. She had heard rumors that when his daughters had been changed to magpies, he'd retreated to a remote island and hollowed out part of a mountainside to protect his girls from their natural predators. No one had ever found his hideaway.

Which meant it would be nearly impossible for anyone to find her. She rested her forehead on her knees and willed her racing heart to slow and the tears gathering behind her eyes to evaporate. She couldn't stop the thought tumbling through her mind that maybe turning into a bird wouldn't be so horrible. At least she'd be able to fly. And Zeus was a far better father than she imagined Pierus to be. Living through eternity as a bird wouldn't completely suck if she could live in Zeus's palace on Olympus.

Who the fuck did she think she was kidding? The idea of being a bird, even in paradise, made her want to punch someone in the throat. She'd start with that son of a bitch,

Pierus.

Footsteps approached from a tunnel she hadn't noticed during her perusal. Someone was coming.

"Ah, our guest is awake, Tyranny." Pierus's sandals scuffed annoyingly on the uneven stone beneath his feet.

Tyranny was perched on his shoulder. Her tiny head had almost completely transformed back to human form, except she still had a beak. Her fingers had completed their evolution back. Bitch still had feathers along her sides that rustled when she flapped her arms.

Pierus stopped in front of the door to the cage and sneered. "You were less of an opponent in this challenge than I thought you'd be, Clio. You made the game too easy."

Glaring at him, she didn't bother to get to her feet. "It's not over yet."

"You're wrong. Your partner has failed his task. The Five Nations Block is advancing on Sofia even now. They can't be stopped."

Resisting the urge to flip a bird of her own in the man's general direction, Clio stood. Before speaking, she smoothed her pants, brushing dust and grit from her behind. When she finished, she crossed her arms over her chest and stared at Tyranny. "If I'd lost, she'd already be real again. But look, she's still locked in the body of a bird."

Pierus narrowed his eyes and blew a breath her direction. Crushing pain gripped her shoulders, trying to push her to her knees on the ground. Clio summoned the most primal of her strengths, her willpower, and remained standing. She turned the power outward and shoved against the force of Pierus's nudge. The demi-god stumbled and tripped on the hem of his toga. Tyranny screeched as she flew from her perch and darted around the room. She finally lit on one of the tree branches. She continued her caterwauling until Clio blasted her with a shut-the-fuck-up command. Her beaky mouth opened and closed several times before she tucked her human head under a wing.

Clio turned her gaze back onto Pierus. The man had tumbled to his ass and was scooting away from her cage. His toga had risen to his thighs as he scuttled along the floor, nearly exposing his junk. She hurled a nudge filled with heat his direction, commanding it to lick along his exposed legs. He jumped to his feet with a girly scream. Which would have made her laugh, but she was too busy being relieved she hadn't caught a glimpse of his shriveled ass.

"You haven't won yet, Pierus. You have some nerve kidnapping and imprisoning me here." Clio lunged forward, reaching for the bars containing her. A fiery burst of pain blazed through her hands when they came in contact with the golden bars. She jerked them back and shook the sting away. "You charmed the cage? You asshole!"

"I needed something to keep you in place while the world plunges into war. The time of man is past. Zeus's reign as a benevolent king and protector of mortals is at an end. My daughters and I will ascend his throne and his office chair over his broken body."

"We'll see." Clio spun around until her back was to him. She didn't want him to see the fear his words had managed to instill.

The cage was charmed, which meant any attempt to communicate with Zeus along their mental link would be futile. She patted the front pocket of her slacks, pleased to feel the firm outline of her cellphone. Once Pierus left the cavern with his shitty daughter, she was going to try to get a more real-world message to Zeus and Jax. She hoped she'd get a signal through all this granite.

Chapter 18

"Found it!" Jax hollered from his position at a laptop. The file the gods had planted on the server took next to no time to locate. Distracting her from Zeke's attentive flirting, he'd pointed out the geological survey from Gaia Engineering to Beryl.

But that one report hadn't been enough to convince the man-eater. She wanted additional proof. Jax argued with her regarding the study's validity. Truly, the report was flawless. No one would ever know it had been manufactured by mythological beings no one believed in. The report contained appropriate longitude and latitude coordinates, as well as core sample reports that exactly matched the make-up of Bulgarian soil in the range where the crystals were located.

While Jax argued his point, over Beryl's shoulder he saw Zeke drop his head back. The man scrubbed a hand over his face, masking the movement of his lips as he communed with the gods. It had been an excellent strategy to have him present.

"What the hell else will it take to convince you, Beryl?" Jax demanded.

"We need more than a simple geological survey. We need a composition report on the crystals," Beryl bitched. "And Burton will never consider it not knowing if these lantern rocks you're all fired up about are, in fact, what The Five Nations is truly after."

Clio had been gone too long. Jax's imagination burned with thoughts of what that shitstain, Pierus, was doing to her. Barely containing his animosity and fear he asked, "What do you think would convince him?"

"A nice tidy paper trail about the role the crystals play in the Block's aggression would be just lovely." The tight smile Beryl sent him was a clear indication of her disbelief he'd be able to produce such a report.

Behind Beryl, Zeke huffed out a breath, shot the bitch a venomous look, and rolled his head in a circle on his neck, once again masking his silent communication.

"I'll find it. You've got some of the best hackers in the business here." Jax pitched his voice toward Zeke. "Tell them to hack into the Kristall Web database in Ukraine. I'm sure we'll find what we need in their secure servers. But we have to act fast."

Zeke opened one eye and nodded at Jax. At least he'd gotten the message.

"Fine." Beryl snapped her fingers. When no one reacted instantly, she slapped her hands together, finally gaining the attention of three techs sitting behind oversize monitors. They stopped pounding the keyboards and paid attention to her. She barked out her orders. "New assignment, boys. We're going fishing in the Kristall Web." She strode away from Jax to give further instructions to the techs.

Jax shoveled agitated fingers through his hair and moved to the window on the opposite end of the room. He battled his growing panic over where Clio might be and what might be happening to her. If he lost her now, it would be worse than when he'd failed at saving the innocents in Sierra Leone. That had been a professional issue. This time it was personal.

He braced his hands on the windowsill and rested his forehead on the glass. Outside rain sluiced from the sky and gale-force winds bent the trees and bushes erratically. The weather had gotten steadily worse in the past few hours. Was it tied to Clio's disappearance? Was this the end Pierus had promised? A week ago, he was worried about baseball scores and what he should eat for breakfast. Now, he believed in gods and goddesses, and the fate of the world weighed heavily on his shoulders.

Zeke joined him at the window. "Hermes has his people on it. They'll put the report somewhere they'll have to dig a little to find, so it doesn't seem like a set-up. Nia's on her way here so she can nudge the tech from close range."

"How long?" Jax asked, pitching his voice low.

"Since Clio vanished? About an hour."

"I know that. How long until Nia gets here?"

"She'll come through the Hollow. Any minute now."

He'd have to remember to ask what the hell the Hollow was when this was all over. "Any progress on finding where they've taken Clio?"

"Not yet." Zeke rested his hand on Jax's shoulder. "I'm sorry, Jax. It's a big, wide world out there. They could be anywhere. Nataero is on it, but it may take a while."

"Who's that?"

"He's in charge of the Lost Things department. Dude can find Waldo anywhere in the world. He'll find Clio."

"Sounds like Olympus is run like a corporation."

Zeke laughed. "Kind of. There are eleven major gods with solid lines directly to Zeus. He's like the CEO. And a slew of dotted lines from the lesser gods. A bunch of broken lines as well. Pierus is on that part of the chart. The ultimate organization chart."

"Will I find an ambrosia station in the employee break room?" Christ, the most inane things went through his mind when he was stressed.

"Nah, man." Zeke thumped his hard abdomen. "That shit will pack on the pounds. We stick to coffee and tea. Zeus even installed Keurig machines in the kitchens.

Personally, I think it's a devious ploy to get everyone back to their desks faster."

Jax started to answer, but his phone vibrated. He consulted the display. "Holy shit!" He shot Zeke a look as he dragged his finger across the screen. "Clio? Where are you? Are you okay?"

"Jax? Thank the goddess." Clio's voice came across as a whisper.

"Are you all right?" Jax angled the phone so Zeke could hear. The man crowded against Jax's shoulder.

"I haven't been turned into a bird yet, but I'd really like to come home." Heavy static garbled her words.

"I want that as well. Zeke's here with me. We don't know where to look for you."

"Zeke? Why is he involved?"

"Long story, Clio. No time to discuss now," Zeke responded. "Do you know where you are?"

"Not really. Pierus threw me into the Hollow, and next thing I knew I was in a cage in a cave. Dipshit Pierus didn't think to take my cell phone. Can you ping it to find me?"

He'd put her in a goddamn cage? Jax was going to kill the fucker when he got his hands on him.

Zeke patted Jax on the back. "Keep her talking." He took a step away from Jax and concentrated on the storm happening outside the window. His lips moved, so Jax was certain he was talking to whatever tech person was on duty on Olympus.

Jax focused back on Clio. "Is there a gate or door to escape through?"

"Yes, but Pierus charmed it. I can't get it open. Jax, the roof of the cavern looks like the kind of granite they mine on Corfu. And I hear waves in the background. There's a good chance I'm on an island somewhere in the Ionian or Adriatic seas."

"Okay, that's good information." Jax twisted until he spied a globe in the corner. As he moved toward it, Beryl glanced at him, as though curious. One of the tech slobs in front of a laptop spoke to her. With a scowl, she dragged her attention back to him.

"Jax, have you made any progress? Have you stopped the Five Nations?"

"Not yet. But with a little help from your dad, we're closer." Jax spun the globe and located the islands off the coast of Greece Clio had mentioned.

"You've met my dad? Damn, I wanted to be there for that meeting."

A brilliant flash of lightning illuminated the room, casting odd shadows everywhere. Thunder boomed immediately after, and the lights dimmed.

"Was that thunder?" Clio asked urgently.

"Yeah. The storm is bad and getting worse. I hope we don't lose power." That would be bad. If they didn't have an Internet connection to get the information they needed, they might not be able to stop the Block's army from marching into Sofia. The death toll could reach over one hundred thousand. And he'd lose Clio. Unacceptable.

"Listen, the library's general system goes down frequently in storms. But the secured mainframe should be okay. Are you plugged into that?"

"I don't know. Dammit, Clio. I'm worried as hell for you. I'm coming to get you as soon as we figure out where you are."

"No! Jax, they need you. You're the only thing standing between me and an eternity as a shitty bird. I'm fine. You stay there and do what's necessary to make sure that doesn't happen."

"Clio—"

"Listen to me, Jax. I'm not cut out to be a bird, so fix this with the Five Nations. But…just in case it can't be fixed, I want you to know I love you."

"I love you, too, Clio. I will fix this, and we will find you." He stared helplessly at the map of the world. They'd better find her. He didn't want to face a future without Clio in it.

Zeke tapped him on the shoulder. "Gotta talk to her." He took the phone from Jax's numb fingers. Zeke whispered. "Clio, Mars is working on getting a location on you. Is your GPS on?"

"Dammit, I forgot to turn it on after the last time I went through the Hollow."

"Get it on! If possible, leave the phone on. Be careful. I'm handing you back to Jax."

Jax stopped scrubbing his hand over his face and took the phone back. "Clio, I'll end this. I'll find a way."

"You better, Jax. I want to look into your eyes when you tell me you love me."

"Same goes, sweetheart."

"Someone's coming. I need to hide the phone. Hurry, Jax."

"Clio!" He shouted into the speaker. The workers popped their heads up and looked his way in a perfect imitation of a prairie dog. They stared for a moment then resumed their work. He cast a frantic glance around the room looking for Zeke.

He located the man talking to a woman with coppery-colored hair and bright blue eyes. Had to be Nia. The family resemblance was unmistakable.

As he stalked across the room to join them, Nia directed her gaze at the drones on the laptops and squinted, an expression Jax knew meant she was nudging them. Her lips moved as she inspired them to find the files that someone on Olympus had planted. When he reached their side, Nia had relaxed against the doorjamb, arms crossed over her chest, a smile tugging the corners of her lips.

Zeke introduced them. "Jax, this is Clio's younger sister, Nia, Muse of Astronomy."

He nodded. "Good to meet you. Did you poke them?"

"Wait for it." Her voice was low with a smoky quality.

She tipped her chin toward the workers. "Should be any second now."

An eternity passed in the five seconds that it took for one of the techs to holler, "I'm in!" The dude's fingers flew over the keyboard as he hacked the Kristall Web mainframe.

Beryl jogged to his side and rested her hand on the back of his chair as she leaned over his shoulder.

The tech leaned forward and slapped his thumb on the space bar. He stared intently at the data flashing on his screen. "Got it!"

"That's it?" Beryl pointed at the monitor. "You're sure?"

The tech nodded and typed a few more keystrokes then clicked his mouse. The printer in the center of the table whirred to life and paper began to spit out. "There's the report."

Beryl seized the pages as they landed in the paper tray. A smile grew on her face. "Somebody get Admiral Burton on the phone."

"And you're welcome," Nia whispered beside Jax. She looked at Zeke speculatively. "So, you're one of us?"

Zeke kept his eye on Beryl and jerked one corner of his mouth up into a crooked half smile. "Long story. But yeah. I work for Zeus as a sort of protective detail."

"Do I have one of you?" she asked.

"Maybe." Zeke redirected their conversation with a nod toward Beryl. "Would you look at the size of her grin? Looks like your plan worked, Jax."

He should have found great satisfaction in saving the world. But his mind was on saving *his* world. "Let's find Clio."

His phone buzzed with a text message. *Congratulations. Meet me in Clio's office. Bring Zeke.* Jax tipped the device so Zeke could read.

"Nia, can you nudge them to not notice I'm gone?" Jax

asked.

"Sure thing."

"Where do you think you're going, Jax?" Beryl's voice followed them down the hall.

Jax spun around, torn between telling Beryl she was on her own and just leaving without a word.

Nia shooed him away. "I've got this. Go save my sister." She turned and squinted at Beryl, stopping the woman in her tracks.

Chapter 19

J ax followed Zeke to the stairwell.
When they arrived at Clio's small office, Zeus was
already waiting for them. This time, he was dressed in
black trousers and a tight black T-shirt. Even his tennis
shoes were black. The get-up was far less unnerving than
the toga he'd worn earlier. "Mars located her beneath a
castle on Corfu."

"Angelokastro?" Jax asked.

"Ah, you know the place?"

"It was an important part of Greece's defense system
in the Byzantine era. Built on a massive cavern. Which is
where Clio said she was being held."

"That's where we are going."

"It will take a day to get there," Jax muttered. Worry
slithered up his spine. Anything could happen in a day.

Zeus's laugh boomed off the ceiling. "Not when you
travel god-style." He laid a hand on each of their forearms.

"Get ready, Jax. It's going to be a wild ride. The
pressure will be crushing. Hold your nose and force air
through your sinuses. Just like you're on a plane." Zeke
demonstrated pinching his nostrils closed.

Zeus nodded encouragingly, urging Jax to mimic Zeke.
Feeling a bit stupid, Jax complied.

The air tightened around Jax's body, compressing to
the point of pain. An ache pounded in the center of his
head. Jax opened his mouth, sucked in a deep lungful of air,

then pursed his lips together and blew hard. His ears popped painfully as the world around him faded to mist.

His traveling companions became mere blobs of light in the monochromatic murkiness surrounding them. Bright cobalt-colored light pulsed in the area where Zeke had stood. Jax dropped his gaze a bit lower and saw a syncopated rhythm beating in the man's chest. Where Zeus had grasped their wrists, light flared under the god's palm. Zeus himself was a bright beacon of purple light, his entire being awash in an aura. He looked like a great big glow stick.

Zeus's voice banged around inside Jax's head. *We will arrive just outside the space where Pierus is holding her. According to Mars, someone is with her. We will be there in a few moments.*

Jax struggled to nod his head. It felt weighted, heavy…as though he was being spun in a centrifuge. Why did mortals ever believe the gods traveled in chariots? This way was definitely faster and more immortal-like. He gave up trying to nod and merely clenched his fist and raised his thumb. His skin glittered silver. The pressure remained steady on his chest, but oddly, he didn't fight to breathe.

His ears popped again, and the world around him morphed back into full color. The floor was six inches below his feet. They floated downward until his soles were planted firmly on the ground. Zeus released their arms and snuck toward an opening in the wall across from them.

From the other side of the gateway, Jax heard the voice he recognized as Peter Russell's, the crazy old dude he'd met on the street a few days ago. The man he now knew as Pierus.

"As long as you are my prisoner, I still hold the upper hand, Clio. I can still turn you into a magpie."

"Not bloody likely," Zeus muttered. "Only I have that power." He put a hand on Jax's arm to still his forward progress.

Jax jerked away. "This ends now."

Zeus waved his hand, freezing Jax in place. The sensation was ten times stronger than the force he'd experienced seconds ago. Breath stalled in his throat. A loud, cackling birdcall echoed from the space ahead.

"A minute, Jax. That is all. We do this my way."

Jax blinked his eyes, the only part of his body that was capable of movement. Zeus smiled, and the pressure on Jax's body eased.

"The Five Nations is negotiating an eleventh hour détente, Pierus. This challenge is over," Clio bluffed.

Zeus pointed to a long, oval mirror located near the entrance. It provided a clear view of the cage where Clio stood. She flung her arm toward the barren tree behind her. "Look, Tyranny is changing back to a bird. You've lost."

"No!"

"Do yourself a favor, Pierus. Release me."

"Never! I may have lost this contest, but I can hold you prisoner for eternity. No one will ever find you here."

"Now," Zeus commanded. He stepped forward and entered the room ahead of them.

Zeke and Jax followed, assuming flanking positions behind Zeus.

Thunder cracked in the room right before Zeus spoke. "Pierus! You will not violate the terms *you* set forth in the challenge. You will release my daughter immediately."

Pierus whipped around to face Zeus, his hands buried in the disheveled curls on his head. "How did you find me? This location is hidden from immortal view. No one has found it for seven thousand years."

"Olympus is a large corporation with many assets. This cave wasn't that difficult to find." He waved his hands toward Clio's cage. He frowned when nothing happened. He lifted one brow and pointed at Pierus. "Remove the charm now before I remove you from this existence."

With a theatrical flair, a spear appeared in Zeus's hand.

The wicked sharp point throbbed with a bluish-white light. He hefted it up until it rested on his shoulders. Spreading his feet apart, he readied to hurl the spear at Pierus if the god didn't obey. Jax stepped around Zeus and headed toward Clio. Eager to free her, he reached toward the bars.

"Stop, Jax!" Clio ordered. She softened her voice. "The bars are charmed. Touching them could kill you."

Jax stilled his arm. Behind the cage, the grotesque magpie squawked. Jax changed direction and stalked to the tree where it perched. The bird flapped its half-human wings, but could not take flight. She jumped toward another branch, but she wasn't fast enough. He seized the stick-like legs. Her feathers scratched as she beat her wings, but Jax didn't release his grip. With his other hand, he covered her head, temporarily blinding it and forcing it to stillness.

Holding the bird in place, he stalked back to Pierus. "Open those gates, or this one dies while you watch." His voice came out tough and gritty.

"Do not hurt her!" Pierus waved his arms toward the gilded cage and muttered in a language Jax recognized as the Ionic dialect of ancient Greek.

Jax roughly translated the incantation as *opening the damn gate*. Something near the locking mechanism fizzed, then the barred gate popped open. Zeus looked at Jax with approval of his ploy to force Pierus to release Clio.

Extending her hand, palm facing the door, Clio cautiously tested the perimeter. She walked through the unlocked gate and moved to Jax's side. Zeus claimed Tyranny from Jax, allowing Jax to spin toward Clio and pull her into his arms. Heaving a relieved sigh, he tightened his arms around the woman who'd become the world to him. Clio buried her face against his chest and wrapped one hand around his neck.

"It's okay. I've got you." Jax smoothed his hand down her back, then pivoted to stand shoulder to shoulder with

Zeus.

Zeke took up a position on Clio's left, creating a line of united determination.

Pierus glared at the four of them. "You think you have won?" He darted his eyes to the bird in Zeus's hands. "You will return my daughter to me this instant and leave my stronghold. You are not welcome here."

Without turning his head, Zeus addressed Clio's bodyguard. "Zeke, please ask Mars if the threat from The Five Nations has been resolved."

Zeke tipped his face toward the ceiling. Thirty seconds passed in silence while Pierus paced in front of their line. When Clio stroked the back of her hand over Jax's, he responded by lacing his fingers tightly with hers. Thirty minutes ago he worried he'd never be able to touch her as a woman again. The contact eased the last amount of fright from his body, leaving love in its place.

Zeke crossed his arms over his muscle-bound chest and leaned his weight on his hip. "All parties have agreed to sit at a table together. The situation is on its way toward resolution. The Bulgarian government is highly interested in the terms GeoPoly put forth. The Five Nations has halted their advance over the border."

Zeus petted Tyranny's feathers. "Then my daughter is successful in this challenge. Pierus, your penalty for challenging the gods in this manner is to forfeit your own daughter."

Pierus lunged forward, his eyes wide. Zeus swept his hand in front of Pierus. The man went unnaturally still. Tears winked in his eyes. "Do not kill her," he begged.

"She will not die. But never again will she live anywhere but on Olympus. It will be her home for all eternity. The same holds true for each of your daughters when you fail in future challenges. After this, you will no longer be allowed to contest their imprisonment."

A wicked light replaced the tears in Pierus's eye. "And

if one of my other daughters is successful? What then?"

"We will abide by the terms of *this* challenge. But hear this, little god." Zeus's voice became thunderous. "The word is already out that I will find all those who help you and punish them as well. And when the challenge is completed, and we have won, I will turn you into a cat and release you in the aviary containing all of your offspring."

Holy hell! Was Zeus going to put Pierus in the position of killing his own children? Jax risked a glance at the stormy face of the king of gods. He was deadly serious about his threat. And judging by the horrified expression on Pierus's face, that little fucker knew it as well.

Zeus firmed his grip on Tyranny and faced Clio and Jax. "Congratulations on your victory, my children." Suddenly, Jax was one of Zeus's children? Clio squeezed Jax's hand as wonder filled his soul.

Zeus continued. "You two may return to Delphi. Zeke, I require your assistance on Olympus." He offered his arm and Zeke rested his hand on it. "We will meet tonight to debrief. Jax, I'd like you to come as well. I will text you the details."

Without releasing her grip on his hand, Clio wove her arm through Jax's and hugged him close. Pressure built in his chest and pain grew in his head. Definitely not his preferred method of transportation. Beside him, Zeus and Zeke vanished. Before Jax and Clio slipped into what they called the Hollow, Pierus raised his fist and shook it at the space Zeus had occupied.

Jax swallowed hard, his ears popped and then Clio dragged him into the misty, gray void.

Chapter 20

C lio blinked them back to her office. Before their feet had touched the ground, Jax had wrapped his arms around her and pulled her close. Never had a man's embrace felt so warm and wonderful. So very right.

She lifted her face to his as she wove her arms around his neck. He slanted his mouth across hers and took her deep into a kiss. Everything had been thrown off-kilter when Pierus had nabbed her. The passion and relief she tasted in Jax's kiss centered her world. And thanks to him, the fate she had been destined for had shifted back to normal.

Jax pulled his lips from hers. "Thank God, you are safe." He snugged her closer against his hard body and rested his cheek on the crown of her head.

"Thank you for saving me." She gave a little laugh. "For saving the world."

"I was so worried. At first Beryl wouldn't even consider the idea of the crystals. My word that the field was there wasn't enough evidence." Jax smoothed his hands along her spine.

"I guess I can see that. And without me there to nudge her around to the idea, you had your work cut out for you."

"Thanks to Zeus, we provided the intelligence Beryl said she'd need to convince Admiral Burton. But even that wasn't enough." He shuddered. "So Zeke informed Zeus of what else was needed. And your dad came through for us."

"About Zeke—"

He quieted her with another lingering kiss. When he drew away, he smiled. "You'll have to ask him. I don't know that much about Zeke's role in your life, but he's a stand-up guy." Jax's eyes gleamed when she leaned back in his arms to look at him.

"You're the first mortal to meet my dad."

"How is that possible? Surely other men you've known have met him. You told me you've been married before."

"They've all known him as merely my father, not the king of gods. You're the first to know him as he actually is."

Jax released her to sit on the edge of her desk. "That doesn't mean I'm doomed or anything, right?"

Goddess, she wished she knew. "Zeus wasn't happy that I'd revealed our existence to you. He mentioned getting Mnemosyne involved."

"Goddess of Memory?"

"You know your mythology." She sat next to him, laying her hand over his where it curled around the edge of the desk. "I think Zeus might be planning to use her to erase your memories about this."

"Can he do that without my consent?"

"Well, he is Zeus. He can pretty much do what he wants." She'd learned a very, very long time ago that it was futile to argue with her dad when he'd made up his mind. "And besides, without your memories, you'd never know it had been done."

Jax tipped his head to the side and looked her in the eyes. "I won't forget about us, will I?

"I don't know. I hope not."

Jax leaned his forehead against hers, holding her gaze, and whispered. "It would be awful if I forget how much I love you."

He'd said it, just as he'd promised. Looked her straight in the eyes and professed his love for her.

Happiness bubbled up like sparkling wine, intoxicating and fresh. "I love you, Jax. Gaia told me that the way my nudges affected you only happens when you share a great love. When you've found the person you are meant to be with through all eternity."

A frown etched lines into Jax's forehead. "Your eternity is a lot longer than mine. Especially if my memory is erased."

The effervescent delight that had coursed through her body went flat. "We won't know what the plan is until later. I've already waited through eight millennia for you. I believe we can wait a couple hours to see what the Fates hold for us."

"Hang on, the Fates are real as well?"

"Of course."

A ray of sunlight beamed through her office window and illuminated a patch of the industrial carpeting that came standard in all the University buildings. "Would you look at that? I feel like this is the first time in a week that I've seen the sun." She angled her head so the light could bathe her cheeks in the warmth.

"I suppose that's a sure sign that we've defeated Pierus. He's beaten, and his accomplices have deserted his cause like rats abandoning a sinking ship."

"I'm sure Zeus has already had words with Guabancex, one of the weather gods." She pressed a kiss to his cheek and then jumped off the desk. "We should probably go check on your team's progress."

She offered him her hand. His palm felt solid and warm against hers when she pulled him to his feet. The sun glinted in his eyes, turning them a luscious shade of amber. His gaze was intent as he drew her into his arms. He dipped his head and claimed her mouth, moving his lips over hers with an unspoken eloquence and simplicity that stole her breath and spoke to her soul. His kiss held passion and promise.

He eased back and spoke against her lips. "I love you, Clio. I will for all time. Even if Zeus decrees my memory must be erased, I swear I will remember you and my love for you."

* * *

The sun had remained out through the rest of the day, drying out the earth. The media had been all aflutter over the last minute agreement between The Five Nations and Bulgaria. Most outlets had proclaimed the sudden treaty a miracle at the very brink of war. Some spoke about the State Department's intervention as authoritative and masterful. The more conservative pundits declared it an act of God.

Clio sat with Jax in the boardroom at Olympus Enterprises and knew it was an act of many gods. This might be her most spectacular feat of altering the course of history. And the greatest source of her inspiration sat next to her with wide eyes. Jax hadn't spoken much since they had arrived at the six-story corporate headquarters on the outskirts of Delphi. He'd gasped when they'd passed through the marble lobby. Jax had clutched her hand in the gilded elevator on the ride to the executive floor.

Clio pointed to an ornate steel door flanked by a massive security station. "That's the door to the Pantheon. Many of our employees have homes on Mt. Olympus, and this is a point of arrival."

Jax let out a low whistle as she ushered him into the luxurious conference room across from the portal. Clio imagined it was a little dizzying to know he was in an office building that was a gateway to the 'mythical' Mt. Olympus.

In the boardroom, the ceiling was painted with frescoes of mortals cavorting and frolicking, the way they did when the gods were happy with them. The paintings had been a source of amusement for Clio since she'd first seen them in the third century. Men might paint gods on their ceilings, but gods painted men.

Callie and Nia had been summoned to the briefing Zeus had arranged. When she'd emerged from the Hollow with Jax, they'd been waiting for her. Almost before her feet touched the ground, both women had hugged her hard and long. They hugged Jax as well, thanking him profusely for saving Clio. Oh, and the world, too.

Jax bounced his knee nervously under the table, barely stopping when she laid her hand on it. "Please don't be nervous, Jax."

"Ha! I'm about to sit through a meeting with beings I've never believed in. Beings I thought storytellers of old had made up to explain the mysterious ways of the universe. Except, what do you know? Not so imaginary after all." His chest heaved as though he was about to hyperventilate.

Clio nudged him, knowing full well the inspiration she blew his way would distract him. His knee stopped bobbing under her palm. He dragged her hand to his lap where she found hard evidence that his thoughts were no longer on the coming meeting. She gave him a big smile, pleased with her ploy.

Zeke entered the room and took a seat between her sisters on the opposite side of the massive black granite table. The slab had come from the quarries of Corfu—a fact Clio found amusing and horrifying. Zeke had traded his security guard uniform for a traditional toga. Callie and Nia wore the formal garb as well. Only Jax and Clio wore mortal clothing.

Clio folded a piece of parchment into a plane and hurled it toward Zeke. "Lucy, you have some 'splainin' to do." She mimicked Desi Arnaz as she spoke. She'd never known the actor, but his antics had entertained her family for hours. Reruns of the Lucille Ball show were one of the things she'd looked forward to when she'd been reborn in this era.

Zeke squirmed in his seat and tried to cover his nervousness by adjusting the drape of his toga over his broad chest. "My father is Itus, the protection god."

She heaved an exasperated sigh. "I know who Itus is, you big goof."

"My purpose is to serve as your partisan, your supernatural bodyguard."

Curiosity overwhelmed her. "How long has this been going on?"

"All your lives."

Clio didn't miss the fact he'd made lives plural. "How? Why?"

"Zeus bestowed the same enchantment on me that you girls all have. I live a mortal existence, but upon rebirth, I come with a full set of memories. And other skills. I come into my powers about a week before you do."

"So you've always protected me? In each lifetime I've known you without knowing about you?"

"My form changes each time I come back. Remember when you were caught in the mob in Constantinople and you were trampled to death?"

One of the drawbacks of being reborn with all your memories intact was that those memories included how you passed away in previous lifetimes. Clio shuddered. It had been an awful moment that had happened so fast she hadn't been able to slip into the safety of the Hollow. She nodded but didn't say anything.

"Zeus was furious with me for letting that happen. Sent me back the next lifetime as a Great Dane." Zeke smiled crookedly.

"Hey, I had a poodle I loved once. Was he a partisan as well?" Nia asked.

"Urania! You ask too many impertinent questions." Callie leaned forward and sent a quelling look toward Nia across Zeke's body. Callie scrunched up her face.

Nia grabbed her neck. "Knock that off. I want to know if we all have protectors."

"Great." Zeke groused. "I'm probably coming back as a gold fish in the next life. All these years of you girls not knowing about partisans, and in one measly day I blow our cover."

Nia gave a victorious shout. "There, you see. There is more than one of him. I wonder if the cute new scientist at the observatory is mine?"

Zeke shook his head and raised pleading eyes toward Jax.

Jax lifted his hands and shrugged. "Can't help you, bro. I'm still reeling from the idea you all actually exist."

Zeke had been there for Clio throughout the ages. She'd even been attracted to him recently. "Have we ever, um…dated?"

Zeke shook his head. "Nope. Not even once. This lifetime was the closest we've ever gotten."

Jax tensed next to her. When she sent him a partial nudge, he gave a small gasp and relaxed.

"Why don't I recognize at least your essence or aura from one life to the next?"

"I am the one memory you don't bring back with you." Zeke shrugged. "Not sure how it works, but honestly, this is the first time I've ever revealed myself to you."

Any further attempt at discussion stopped dead when the door swept inward. Zeus strode in, a contingent of people following closely behind. Everyone at the table stood in respect.

"Good evening, daughters." He moved around to the other end of the room and took the throne-like seat at the head of the table. He nodded toward Jax. "Good to see you again, son."

That was the second time her father had referred to Jax in familial terms.

Gaia slipped into the space next to Clio. Her mother's embrace was tight and fierce. She whispered into Clio's ear, her breath tickling. "I am so delighted you aren't a bird."

Clio laughed. "Me, too."

Gaia released her and then offered her hand to Jax. "I am Gaia, Clio's mother."

"Pleasure to meet you, um, Gaia." Jax took her hand, but looked uncertain as to whether he should shake it or kiss the back of it. He darted a glance at Clio, his eyebrows raised.

Gaia resolved the issue for him when she pumped his hand up and down with a grin. "Thank you for saving my daughter."

"Enough pleasantries, woman!" Impatience edged Zeus's powerful voice. He dropped into his chair. "Everyone take a seat, please."

Once all the occupants had settled, Zeus rapped the table with his knuckles. Sound cracked around the room, and everybody sat a little straighter.

"Jax, allow me to introduce you. To your left is Mars from Security. At the other end of the table is Hermes. He is in charge of communications. And lastly"—Zeus gestured to the god on Callie's right—"we have Hephaestus, my executive assistant. Gentlemen, Jax Callahan, history professor."

Jax lifted a hand. All the gods inclined their heads in greeting. Hermes placed his winged helmet in front of him on the table. The door burst open, and a frazzled looking man Clio recognized as the God of Marriage stumbled into the room. Mnemosyne strolled sedately behind him. Clio tensed and reached for Jax's hand. She leaned toward him, seeking his body heat, as all of hers seemed to have fled at the sight of her aunt. Zeus was going to erase Jax's memory.

Ignoring Mnemosyne, Zeus frowned at the other man.

"You are late, Hymenaios."

"Pardon, my lord. I had trouble with a bride."

"Why is he here?" Clio demanded.

"Silence, daughter. In good time. First let us discuss Pierus and what we've learned from this challenge."

"We learned that getting kidnapped and stuck in a cage sucks worse than pond scum," Clio scoffed.

"Be serious, Clio." Callie's hiss was proof that her heartfelt *I love you* from earlier had succumbed to time limits visible only to her.

Zeus extended a calming hand toward Callie. "Anyone else have an observation?"

"We can be certain Pierus does not work alone. This time it was the gods of weather who aided him." Leaning forward, Mars tapped a pen on the table. "No telling whom he'll enlist next time. This challenge he has issued is little more than a ploy to dethrone you, Zeus."

All around protests went up. Zeus hushed them all simply by raising his eyebrow. "I agree with Mars. He has always exalted himself as higher than the rest of the gods. He would use his daughters to win control of Olympus."

"Then, at all costs, we must stop him." Determination laced Gaia's tone.

Clio spoke up. "Zeus, will you really turn Pierus into a cat?"

"I believe I will. Or maybe a mouse and let his daughters eat him. Either way, once all nine of you have faced her foe, we must end his existence." He directed his gaze at Callie. "Have you heard any more from him?"

Callie shook her head. "I believe we might have a brief respite before the next challenge. He'll need time to regroup."

"I concur." Mars crossed his arms over his chest, revealing the tattoo depicting the Acropolis. "It is what I would do."

"If this is the consensus, we will table the topic for

now." Zeus scanned the gods seated around. His gaze finally lighted on Jax. He asked, "What shall we do with this mortal?"

"He knows too much." Hermes stated. "You won't be able to keep him from spilling this secret. It would be a logistical nightmare. Best to let Mnemosyne do her thing."

"No!" Clio's reserve splintered. "You can't take him away from me."

"Clio, it's okay," Jax said as he tightened his grip on her hand. "I found you before. I'll find you again. We can be together without me remembering all of this. Besides, you'll remember us and can chase me until you catch me."

"Mnemosyne, is there a way you can take away Jax's memory of our existence but leave his remembrance of Clio intact?" Gaia asked.

"No. It will not work that way," her auntie responded. "All memory of the truth of gods and goddesses would be erased. I do not offer an à la carte menu."

"It is as I thought." Zeus lowered his chin to his chest.

Mnemosyne rose and moved to Jax's side. She rested her hand on the crown of his head.

"No!" Clio burst out of her seat and knocked Mnemosyne's hand from Jax's head. She shoved her aunt backward then held her in place with a powerful nudge. Jax surged to his feet next to her.

Pain pinched her own neck as Zeus tossed a nonverbal command to her. She resisted, something she'd never done before. She'd always obeyed her father. Always done as he'd asked. In this, she would be defiant. She wouldn't allow him to wipe out the memories of the love of her life. Of all her lives. Callie and Nia scurried around the table and took up positions on each side of her.

Nia grinned. "Hope we don't end up grounded over this."

"Release her, Clio." Zeus's nudge came harder.

She wasn't able to maintain her nudge on Mnemosyne

and resist her father's hard push. She dropped her hand. Defeated tears leaked from the corner of her eyes. She turned to face Jax and slipped into his arms, burying her face in his chest.

His heart beat strongly under her cheek. What would her life be like if he didn't love her back after they stole his memory? Dread seeped like cold, clawing dampness through her body. Her entire future, her eternity, would forever be bleak knowing she hadn't been with this man in at least this lifetime. Calming her with the repetitious motion, Jax smoothed his hand over her hair.

Clio heard the legs of her father's chair scrape the floor. She turned her face from him, refusing to look at the man who would steal her happiness. Wrapping her arms more tightly around Jax, she attempted to blink them into the Hollow away from the boardroom.

Her attempt flickered and died. Dammit, someone had charmed the room to keep her from escaping with Jax.

Behind her, Zeus whispered. She couldn't make out his words, but the sudden swishing of fabric indicated movement. Mnemosyne moved into her field of vision as she made her way to the door. When she exited the room, Zeus moved in front of Clio. She lifted her head, a question in her heart.

"I can see how important this man is to you, Clio. My preference would be to remove his memories. It would be easier and cleaner. I could orchestrate a meeting between you two to ensure you are together in this lifetime. But in the end, when you are reborn and Jax isn't, your memories of him will break your heart."

"I'll take whatever time I can get with her, sir." Jax firmed his grip around her shoulders.

"Father, please. If you must erase his knowledge of our existence, please…" She didn't know how to finish her plea. Which would be worse? A broken heart now before she had a chance to love him more? Or the anguish of having loved him in this lifetime but facing eternity with only the memory of him that never faded?

"Gaia and I have discussed this. She told me of how your nudges have affected him."

Heat flashed into her cheeks as she glared over her shoulder at her mother. Gaia's face remained a placid mask. But a curious light danced in her eyes. Clio drew her brows together but turned to face Zeus.

"What if I fix it so you two can be together forever?" Zeus's question came whispery soft, as if for her ears only.

Hope clawed up in Clio's soul and stood alongside despair. "How would you do this?"

"If Jax is agreeable, I will bestow on him the same gift of rebirth that Zeke possesses. Except you will recognize Jax in the future. Once you come into your powers, he will return to your life."

"You can do this?" Clio's voice rose with her excitement.

"Daughter, I am Zeus. King of the Gods. I can do whatever I will." Zeus's laugh bounced off the faces of the mortals painted on the ceiling.

"I'll do it!" Jax exclaimed.

Clio turned to face him. Love lit his eyes with an incandescent glow. She bit her lip as she studied his face. "Are you sure?"

He glanced toward Zeke. "It's not going to hurt, is it? Accepting the gift?"

A crooked smile moved over Zeke's face. "Nah, bro. You won't even notice a difference."

Jax returned his gaze to Clio's face and cupped her cheek. "Even if it hurt like a gunshot to the heart, I'd do it for you. I want to be with you forever. I love you, Clio. If this is how we can be together and remember every instant of our time, then yes, I will accept this gift."

Tears brimmed in her eyes, but a smile stretched her lips wide as Jax pressed a kiss to her mouth.

Zeus cleared his throat. "Step aside, Clio," he instructed.

Once Clio moved away, Zeus waved his hands over Jax's body. Humor lurked in his tone when Zeus spoke. "Done. I bet you didn't feel a thing."

"Wait, that's it? No words, no booming thunder or clashes of lightning?" Clio narrowed her eyes at Zeus.

The immortal spread his hands wide and smirked. "Nothing quite so dramatic. But Jax is now one of us. We'll leave you alone."

He grasped Jax's forearm and dragged him forward. He lowered his voice enough for only Clio and Jax to hear. "Do not make my daughter unhappy. In this lifetime or any others. I can still turn you into a mouse and let you loose in Tyranny's cage." He pounded his fist on Jax's back. "By the way, Hymenaios will be waiting outside the door. Just in case."

Jax shot a look across the room at the beaming face of the God of Marriage. "Give me a minute to ask, will you?"

"Already disrespecting the father-in-law? I might have to change my mind." Zeus's laughter belied his words.

He leaned his forehead against Clio's. "He will be a good addition to our family." He turned and shooed everyone from the room.

Gaia took his spot when he moved aside. For a change, as she pressed her forehead to Clio's, her eyes remained open and staring. And she wasn't silent. "I hope this solution is the one you desire."

"It is." Clio pressed her cheek to Gaia's. The woman could be a stiff and unyielding goddess when she wanted, but at the moment, she was just a mom.

Zeus took Gaia's hand, tucked it into the crook of his elbow, and escorted her from the room.

Jax rested his hands on Clio's shoulders and pulled her back to his chest. From behind her, he wrapped his arms around her waist, and she stroked her fingertips over the muscles exposed by his rolled-up sleeves. His heart pounded beneath her spine, in perfect sync with hers.

She leaned her head back until it rested in the curve between his neck and chest. "It's too late to change your mind. You're stuck with me for all eternity now. I promise to beat you at *Call of Duty* for the rest of our lives together."

His laughter rumbled in his chest. "You can try." He nibbled the crest of her ear and then spread kisses along her cheek. "I promise to not ask too many questions about different periods in history that fascinate me."

She spun in his arms to face him. "I promise to love you in this lifetime and every one to follow, Jax."

"I'll hold you to that promise and return it with every fiber of my heart. I love you, Clio." He bent his head to hers and whispered against her lips. "What do you say we invite Hymenaios back into the room?"

"A great idea. Yes, Jax. Now and forever, yes."

Keep reading for more of
the Goddesses of Delphi

Mayhem

Coming Nov 8, 2016

A freak solar flare plunges Nia Thanos, Muse of Astronomy, into an evil immortal's attempt at a hostile take over of Olympus Enterprises. Her jobs—save the family business while rescuing the world from pandemonium. To eliminate the menace she must convince one mortal man to believe in the magic of *what if*.

'Doubting Thomas' Wilde hosts a television program aimed at busting myths. But when Nia confesses to being a Muse, it's one myth he can't bust, or believe. His refusal to help leaves Nia to face the challenge on her own.

Riots, looting, and general anarchy are minor problems compared to what's coming if the balance of power shifts on Olympus. Nia's undeniable attraction to Thomas wreaks havoc on her heart and threatens her ability to secure the safety of humankind. Nia finds herself fighting to persuade the one man she can't live without to help save the world.

Chapter 1

The hard metal railing of the platform dug into Nia Thanos's hip when she leaned against it. She shifted to a more comfortable spot and adjusted the focuser on the Helios Institute's long-range telescope. Putting her eye to the eyepiece, she zeroed in on the satellite jetting across the heavens. The sky was clear enough to make out individual stars. A meteor streaked across the top of the field of vision. Through the powerful scope she could make out the Hinomaru emblazoned on the side of the satellite. Japan's circle of the sun.

Checking the time on the digital readout, Nia smiled when she determined the communications spacecraft had lost fifteen seconds on its orbital timetable. She made a time notation on a clipboard attached to the desk-like platform. Her counterpart at the Japanese Space Agency would have to be told one of their thrusters appeared to be failing.

Now, to figure out how to explain to them how she knew exactly what the problem was. It wasn't like she was a rocket scientist. She couldn't even begin to explain to them why an observatory manager would know about the mechanical workings of a foreign piece of space junk orbiting the earth.

They'd think she'd gone off the deep end if she straight out told them she was a Muse.

Older than time. Smarter than the average scientist. Personally acquainted with the mortal known as Galileo. Yeah, the guy known as the father of observational astronomy.

Nia did a quick review of which American Space Agency scientist to share the information with. It would be easy enough to suggest to someone susceptible to her brand of influence that the hurtling sputnik needed an adjustment.

"Nia?"

She turned to see Bradley ambling into the cavernous observatory room. He halted in the rectangle of mid-afternoon sunlight streaming in through the open portal. The ends of his hair winked with golden highlights in the bright light.

She sent him a smile. "What's up?"

"The Campfire Scouts are here. For their tour."

"Oh, fiddle. Is that today?" How had she forgotten another tour?

"I can show them around them if you want." The offer of assistance came with a smile. "I have nothing else on my schedule."

Nia moved across the decking on the platform, her footfalls echoing off the girders supporting the rounded ceiling. "Nah, I've got this. The little nippers usually have interesting questions." She climbed down the steps. "You are certainly welcome to join, if you wish. Always nice to have your creative brand of wit along for these things."

Crossing the room, she made her way to the small table by the door. She took a quick slurp from the drink she'd left there when she'd come into the room. The sugary beverage hit her system with a burst of energy and vigor.

She picked up her smartphone and did a quick check of her email. Still nothing from her sister, Callie, regarding the challenge they faced from Pierus. The presumptive demi-god had surfaced recently and resurrected his daring attempt to free his imprisoned daughters and conquer the world. Starting with her family's corporation, Olympus Enterprises.

Clio, another of her eight sisters had faced the trial last month, and been successful. Now, the first of Pierus's disgusting magpie daughters, Tyranny, was safely locked in the aviary on Olympus. Tension had grown to monumental proportions as they waited to see which of Pierus's daughters would be unleashed next, and which Muse would be chosen to respond.

For now, Nia subscribed to the idea that no news was good news. It was wishful thinking to hope that after his last defeat, Pierus had abandoned his quest to free his daughters from the punishment Zeus had decreed thousands of years ago. Being magpies suited those bitches. In the meantime, all of the Thanos sisters waited and remained vigilant.

Glancing at the bank of world clocks on the far wall, Nia was shocked to discover she'd been in the observatory for three hours. She always lost track of time when gazing at the cosmos.

"Maybe after the tour, you'd agree to go get that drink we've been talking about for the better part of the month." Hope flourished in Bradley's tone.

More like the drink she'd been avoiding for the better part of the month. He was a nice guy, but she wasn't in the least bit attracted to him. And never would be. Head down, she scanned her email messages while mumbling, "You have an appointment you've forgotten about."

Bradley snapped his fingers. "Wait, I forgot I have a session with my personal trainer tonight."

Success! "Oh, guess that drink will have to wait for some other time." Nia didn't know why she didn't just tell him she wasn't interested. Maybe because she hated any form of rejection herself. Had for the entire millennia. In each lifetime, this type of situation had come up. She used to be better at telling people no.

Through the open door, the high pitch squealing of a gaggle of young girls reached the usually quiet confines of the telescope room.

Bradley looked over his shoulder toward the noise filtering in through the open doorway. "We better get going before they shriek the roof down."

Nia silenced the phone and then slipped it into the back pocket of her jeans. As she walked toward the exit, she double-checked she had her nametag on. She did, but it was upside down. A quick flick of her wrist and she righted it. Bradley dogged her heels as she moved toward the steadily increasing sound of little girls shrieking.

A group of girls dressed in identical navy shorts and white blouses waited in the octagonal lobby. All but one had a red kerchief knotted around their necks. The large central room was one of Nia's favorite at Helios. The ceiling was midnight blue with maps of the constellations depicted in phosphorescent paint that glowed at night when the lights had been dimmed. In the center of the room, a recessed area held a mammoth replica of the Earth. The globe rotated in the manner of the real planet, making a full circuit each hour. Strategically placed lights shifted from day to night as the globe spun. It was surrounded by limestone railings. Visitors typically clustered around the observation area and checked the position when they first entered.

The good-sized group of uniformed eight-year-olds stood at the rail, pointing and gesturing as the orb spun slowly on its axis. The group leaders clustered to one side, keeping a watchful eye on their young charges.

Nia made her way to the adults. "Hello, and welcome to Helios."

"I'm Peggy Dartmoor, group leader. Thank you for hosting us today." A woman in yoga pants and a Spandex top extended her hand, offering Nia a limp handshake.

Nia resisted the urge to adjust her hand in the girly

grasp and tighten her grip. Instead, she settled for a toothy smile. "We love to have groups of impressionable kids visit. We never know when we might influence someone to be the next Sally Ride." The astronaut was one of Nia's greater triumphs. The first American woman in space had started out wanting to be a professional tennis player.

The vacant look on Peggy's face indicated she might not know whom Nia was talking about. The woman's blond ponytail slapped against her shoulder when she jerked her head to the side. "Bridget, you stop that this instant."

Nia followed the woman's sharp glance to discover a little imp attempting to crawl over the railing onto the globe. Same blond hair, same skinny build. Most likely they were mother and daughter.

Clapping her hands together, Nia raised her voice and began the process of herding cats. "Here now. Why don't we step into the classroom?" She nodded to Bradley, who led the way across the lobby. The troop followed like giggly lemmings.

The little girl not wearing the kerchief attached herself to Nia's side, instead of hanging out with her friends. The cherub, a halo of glittery golden curls surrounding her face, sent her a shy smile. "My name is Hailey. What's yours?"

"I'm Nia."

"It's very nice to meet you, Ms. Nia."

The child's manners and mature demeanor should have charmed the socks right off Nia. But kids and her didn't mix well. Never had. "Pleasure to meet you as well, Hailey. Have you been to the observatory before?"

The kid snuck her small hand into Nia's. "My uncle brought me here last week to see the Per...Per..." she paused and squinted. "Persnickety shower."

Nia grinned. "The Perseid meteor shower?" The spectacular celestial display occurred every August. The observatory always drew a huge crowd for that. Crowds made her tense, but so did children. Nerves tightened along

Nia's shoulders. She attempted to disengage her hand from the child's before she broke out in a sweat. Hailey gripped her tighter.

The long blond curls jiggled when the girl nodded her head vehemently. "That's it! Did you see me?"

"There were a lot of people here that night." Nia tossed a frantic glance around for Bradley, spying him already in the classroom ahead. She pointed him out to Hailey as they crossed into the large dimly lit room. "Um, Mr. Bradley can help you find a seat. Why don't you run along and ask him."

The child lifted her eyebrows and made sad eyes at Nia. Sucking her bottom lip between her teeth, she dropped Nia's hand, and tucked hers behind her back. *This is what it feels like to have to reach up to scratch a snake's belly.* Shame flamed around Nia's chest.

She relented. "Listen, Hailey. Maybe you'd like to sit up front while I'm talking?"

"Can I?" Her voice had lost the notes of excitement it had held earlier.

Goddess, she landed in the soup this time. She'd hurt this little girl's feeling simply because young children made her uncomfortable. Stupid phobia. She was a freaking Muse, meant to inspire others toward greatness. Well, who the Hades was going to inspire her to be more comfortable around children? If her gift worked on kids this age, she'd mentally message Hailey to go attach herself to Bradley, or one of the other Campfire Scouts. But, except in rare occurrences, children under a certain age were not susceptible to suggestion.

Too damn bad, as far as Nia was concerned.

"Sure, come on," she told Hailey. "I have rock star seating down in front."

"I have to sit on a rock?" Hailey tipped her head to the side, a quizzical smile on her face.

Note to self—kids take everything literally. Nia

touched the child on the shoulder, aiming her toward the front of the small auditorium. Bradley was already passing out the age-appropriate take-home packets they'd designed and prepared for visiting school groups.

Nia left her little shadow in the center seat and walked up the two steps to the raised platform reserved for staff and visiting lecturers. She drew a deep breath and addressed the eager little faces assembled in front of her. "Welcome to the Helios Institute, home of Delphi's world-renowned observatory and planetarium. If you've been here before, please raise your hand."

Ten small hands shot into the air, fingers wiggling. The volume of chatter escalated until Peggy shushed everyone, waving her arms wildly at the girls, a massive scowl on her face.

Nia wasn't bound by age restrictions as far as Peggy was concerned, so she directed a stare at the woman and muttered under her breath, "You look quite tired. You want to sit down." Satisfaction rippled in her ribcage when Peggy yawned and dropped into a seat right next to her mini-me, Bridget.

Nia continued her talk about the facility, gearing the words and tone to the eight-year-olds, not worrying about whether the parents were bored. There was a lot to discover at Helios, regardless of their age.

Clicking the remote that operated the electronics in the room, Nia dimmed the lights and began the laser show that projected various constellations on the ceiling. The professionally narrated show about how the star groupings were named lasted only a few minutes and the audience applauded when it was all done.

Bringing the house lights back up, Nia couldn't help but notice the chagrined look on Hailey's face.

The child waved her hand in the air. "Ms. Nia?"

"Did you have a question, Hailey?"

"Uncle Thomas said the stories are all made up. Those

people the constellations were named for never existed."

"We call them myths, but usually, stories like this are handed down from age to age, and might have some basis in true life." Nia knew most of the tales behind the information accompanying the light show were factual accounts. She'd lived through all of them. "But you can choose to believe or not. It's up to you."

"Thomas says not to believe in anything you can't see or touch."

What the heck kind of uncle turns a kid into a jaded skeptic by the third grade? Nia started to argue, but changed her mind. Getting into it with a kid in front of a bunch of other kids would only end in disaster. "Okay, then. Let's continue our tour."

Bradley herded the youngsters out of the small theater. Several of the Campfire Scouts grouped together, alternately whispering behind their hands and pointing back toward Hailey. Nia was certain the cornerstone philosophy of the Scout organization was to be a decent human being. Someone should give the little stinkers the definition of what kindness entailed.

Hailey hung back, crowding next to Nia, as though afraid to catch up with her troop-mates. Nia let her, but kept her own hands in her pockets to make sure Hailey didn't have the opportunity to cling too closely to Nia.

The girls giggled and the accompanying moms gossiped instead of paying attention to the details of the tour. Resentment simmered in Nia as the entire group grew more distracted. She had many more important things to do than spending time with disrespectful women who should be setting an example for their daughters.

She never liked unleashing her unique brand of persuasion on people who were focused only on the importance of being them. Individuals like that truly couldn't be inspired to think of bigger pictures. Typically they had no interests beyond the tiny universe where they played the sun and everyone else orbited around them. It would be useless to try to nudge the inattentive chaperones to tune in to what the institute was all about. She didn't believe in wasting of her energy.

So rather than send them a mental shut-the-fuck-up command, she cleared her throat quite loudly. It worked in gaining their attention. "We're about to enter the observatory. Each of you will have a chance to look through the telescope to see the stars."

"Ms. Nia?" Hailey spoke up. Her brown eyes were over-large in her face. "It's daytime. How will we see the stars?"

It was something usually asked by the adults. "Excellent question. Even though it is day here, the stars are still out. Because they are a long, long way from Earth, the light from the sun dims their twinkle during our daytime. With my super-duper telescope, we'll be able to see all the way to where they are in space. The stars will look like big points of light in the dark blue sky."

"My mommy and daddy are stars now."

Nia paused as she reached for the handle to pull the heavy steel door open. That sounded like something you'd tell a grieving child. Unsure of how to respond to the girl, she continued opening the door to the observatory.

Her pride and joy—her baby—stood dead center in the massive space. The barrel of the larger refracting scope extended twenty feet from the edge of the viewing platform. A smaller version was piggybacked above it. The entire structure dominated the room and was focused on a section of the sky Nia knew would be visible at this time of day.

Bradley organized the kids in a line at the foot of the viewing platform while Nia hurried up the steps with a wooden box the youngsters could stand on to look through the viewer. She double-checked the sharpness of the image visible in the eyepiece, twisting the focus knob to better define the edges.

She straightened and looked at the line of expectant faces at the foot of the stairs. Pointing to the first child, she said, "Okay, come on up."

One by one, the children all took turns, with the chaperones mixing in. Nia relished the chorus of oohs and aahs as they spied the celestial objects millions of miles away. Once the last person took their turn the tour was officially over. Nia and Bradley escorted the group back to the main lobby, where parents waited to retrieve their kids. Bradley hustled out of the area without as much as a glance over his shoulder, leaving Nia alone with the dissipating crowd.

The last remaining child was Hailey, who stood forlornly next to Peggy and Bridget Dartmoor. Peggy heaved a deep sigh and checked the time on her phone. "Hailey, your uncle is coming, isn't he? He's late. I have to take Bridget to ballet class."

"He should be here. What if something bad happened to him?"

Now that the tour was officially over, Nia had intended to return to her office. The panic in the child's voice punched her gut like a fist. She might not be the most nurturing woman alive, but she couldn't leave the frightened young girl.

Peggy crossed her arms under her chest, exaggerating her already awesome cleavage. "The only bad thing that's going to happen to him is me yelling at him for being late." She shook her head and muttered, "It'd be easier to get mad if he was ugly as sin."

Nia started to laugh, and quickly hid her reaction behind a cough. Peggy might have thought she was quiet, but Nia had enhanced hearing, part of the territory for being a Muse. Not much escaped her.

And suddenly, she was intrigued by the idea of seeing what Hailey's uncle actually looked like.

The entrance door burst open and a man raced through. He paused just inside, doing a rapid scan of the area. When he caught sight of their little group, his smiling gaze zeroed in on Hailey. Nia felt a sharp pang in her chest. Her breath shortened as the intensity of the man's grin brightened the shadowy lobby. His longish blond hair swept the collar of his cobalt T-shirt. Black jeans rode low on his lean waist. The leather flip-flops on his feet finalized his surfer look. As Hailey hurtled toward him, he stooped low to catch her. The denim of his jeans hugged his powerful thighs in a way that made Nia's mouth water.

Definitely not as ugly as sin.

About The Author

Gemma's favorite desk accessories for many years were a circular wooden token, better known as a 'round tuit,' and a slip of paper from a fortune cookie proclaiming her a lover of words; some day she'd write a book. All it took was a transfer to the United Kingdom, the lovely English springtime, and a huge dose of homesickness to write her first novel. Once it was completed and sent off with a kiss, even the rejections addressed to 'Dear Author' were gratifying.

After returning to America, she spent a number of years as a copywriter, dedicating her skills to making insurance and the agents who sell them sound sexy. Eventually, her full-time job as a writer interfered with her desire to be a writer full-time and she left the world of financial products behind to pursue an avocation as a romance author.

To learn more about Gemma and her works, or to subscribe to her newsletter visit:

Website and Blog
http://www.gemmabrocato.com
Facebook
https://www.facebook.com/gemma.brocato
Twitter:
https://twitter.com/GemmaBrocato
Goodreads
https://www.goodreads.com/author/show/7229886.Gemma
_Brocato

Newsletter Sign Up

Sign up for Gemma's Newsletter for updates, exclusive content, new release information, cover reveals and more.

http://eepurl.com/54Kqj

www.ingramcontent.com/pod-product-compliance
Lightning Source LLC
Chambersburg PA
CBHW020949180626
46814CB00003B/1000